ALSO BY GLORIA VANDERBILT

Once Upon a Time: A True Story

Black Knight, White Knight

THESE ARE BORZOI BOOKS
PUBLISHED IN NEW YORK BY
ALFRED A. KNOPF

NEVER SAY
GOOD-BYE

Gloria Vanderbilt

NEVER SAY
GOOD-BYE

A NOVEL

Alfred A. Knopf   New York

1 9 8 9

Library of Congress Cataloging-in-Publication Data
Vanderbilt, Gloria, [date]
Never say good-bye / Gloria Vanderbilt.
p.   cm.
ISBN 0-394-57155-X
I. Title.
PS3572.A42828N48   1989
813'.54—dc20   89-45301   CIP

To
Anne V. Hartwell
with love

NEVER SAY
GOOD-BYE

Jess

My name is Jess, Jessica actually, Jessica Willis Weatherbee, and as I lie here in the sun, Labor Day weekend, terrace, New York City (you get the picture), a phone from somewhere starts ringing, jangling into serious musings I've taken to having lately revolving around my lover, Maclin Hollis, and his feisty wife, Billie, who hangs in there like a lockjawed terrier. (In my bitchy moments I call her Bill.) Why I put up with his coming in and going out of my life as he has over the years is a question I put to myself from time to time, and preoccupied as I am with these matters, it doesn't seep through to me that it's my private phone (a number only he has) that's ringing. Just as I pick it up, it stops. Of course I can't call him back—and there they are again, the dots and flashes like signals from outer space, heralding a migraine.

It's been fifteen days since I last saw him. Not that he's inattentive; he calls every day, twice sometimes, from wherever he is. Work takes him all over, hopping and jumping around here and there, and I keep telling myself that when you come right down to it Billie sees less of him than I do, because when he is here he spends most of his time with me. He's a TV journalist, a sort of latter-day Ed Murrow, very successful in his work (so am I), and when we are together it's one big long time in bed, with catching up for a half hour or so later and then a taxi on our way to wherever we're going. He insists I drop him off first (unless he's heading for Kennedy), because it gives us more time together, then he gives me money for the cab (always too much) and off he goes. There's much turning around and waving to each other as away the taxi lurches, and it's only later that I realize (forgive the cliché) I feel like they say you're supposed to feel after a Chinese dinner: only half full. Oh well—there's next time, I tell myself, and there always is, ever since we set eyes on each other and fell for each other on the spot. At the time it never occurred to me that he was married. An eccentric loner was what I thought—that is, when I had wit to think—and actually it isn't too off the mark, only, married he is. I'm not. My husband, Abe, died fifteen years ago, and since then I've managed to run the Weatherbee Galleries with continuing success. Before Mac, married men were off limits, always had been. Not that I judged anyone else; I just knew that with my temperament I couldn't handle it, ending up in a long tunnel waiting for the phone to ring, no tomorrow, only today—you know, things like that. It went against the hopes I had for myself. So now why am I in that very darkness, with images presenting themselves in kaleidoscope patterns, juxtaposed one upon the other . . . scenarios, but which one is the winner?

.   .   .

SCENARIO ONE: Having just departed after a particularly lustful afternoon, as usual he turns to wave one last time. Instead of leaning out the window, blowing kisses, I turn away, but not before I see his face. Baffled, he pauses, then runs after the taxi as it pulls away . . . Hostile on my part, isn't it, but that's because we had a tiff on the phone just now—*impossible* sometimes, he really is.

SCENARIO TWO: "Jessa?" he says. He's called me that from the beginning—no one else ever has. "Jessa, you know I want to live with you—sooner or later I'm going to leave her . . ." We're on the way out the door, and that stricken look I recognize changes his face and I reach up to touch it.

"Mac!" I call out, and he pulls me toward him and it's happening all over again though it's late and we were about to leave. The chair's lumpy but feels nice, and it's not until later I remember how he threw the pillow on the floor and that when we finally left, snow was falling and it took a long time to find a taxi . . . Only now, as this passes before me, do I remember that it really did happen.

The Weatherbee Galleries are in a gray-stone house off Fifth Avenue, and the warehouse is downtown. The latter's a serviceable building, with three rooms on the top floor that Abe used as offices. For a long time I couldn't bring myself to go there, but now I do because that's where Mac and I meet. It's more like a place to live in than an office. Abe and I planned it so and used to spend weekends there together, just the two of us, when Katie was visiting her grandma. It's strange to think of it now as what Mac calls "our place."

SCENARIO THREE: I'm on my way to the airport to meet him in London. Hours have been spent with my friend Felice, trying to decide what will cram into the duffel now jiggling along on the seat beside me: white silk dress (washable), ditto skirt, white camisole, blouse to double as jacket, sandals, filigree silver belt. Make-up basics, but space at the last minute for large-size Laszlo soap. Yes, set for any occasion. But am I? On the plane, trembling, unable to sleep, remembering how sometimes, extravagantly, he takes a handful of hair from the back of my head, gives it a yank—the fierce tenderness in this that almost hurts . . . The impatient elegance in the way his head moves when he turns suddenly, other things too, things he has no idea I notice about him, obsess me. At Heathrow, there he is in the distance, coming closer—but it's someone I don't know. I stand there waiting, wondering if he's going to show up.

Ah yes! those countless hours Felice and I have spent debating what to pack into that famous duffel for those trips to those places he insists we meet, those trips that may be canceled at the last minute. Summer places and winter places, not to mention the in-between places, Milwaukee and Detroit kind of places. On the bedpost Felice and I have hung all seasonal possibilities, discussing for hours the pros and cons of each before zeroing in on the dandy essentials.

. . .

SCENARIO FOUR: Paris, Ritz Hotel: I brush aside the taffeta curtains . . . pearly the light as I look into the garden below, leaning over the balcony, soft the rain as it grazes my face. He turns in sleep and the puff from the brass bed slides to the floor. Eerily, the twilight-dawn reminds me of other times, of after-noons in other rooms when he has turned from me. But now there is a permanence in the way his arm sprawls across the pillow, in the way his hand fans upward in an abandonment to trust. After all, we have had five days together, five days which will not end until tomorrow, as if we really do have a life together (which of course we don't). Suddenly the rain stops, and sparrows call back and forth to each other. My eyes close as his arms enfold me . . . Sweetness, he says, and we stand looking down at someone who has come out to putter among the hydrangea pots, while across the courtyard a window opens, a woman draws a kimono around her, moves back into the shadows. As he pulls me toward the bed, something in me is lost, irreversibly . . . belongs now only to him.

SCENARIO FIVE: Taking pen in hand, I write: Mac, sometimes I don't feel I really get through to you (except in bed, of course—which I may add is the *best*). Still there are things I want to say to you in answer to the times when you have said to me that "sooner or later" you are going to leave Billie, that you are miserable with her and were for a long time even before we met. I know you dread "the confrontation," as you put it, having to make the move (so to speak) and face her, and so the days and months slip by into years and it gets more impossible for all concerned. Your children can't help but be aware of what's going on (have been for years). So's Katie, of course. And it's too late now for Billie to threaten to take Jenny away from you to Indiana (the way she used to). Are you afraid they'll stop loving you? You don't *really* believe that, do you? What I'm trying to say is that I'm in love with you and have been since the moment we met, though now I'm not only in love with you—I love you. You keep saying you want to live with me— Darling, what do I have to do to get through to you? We don't have to get married, though someday, if you ever asked me, guess what I'd say? I hope in time your children will come to be friends with me. Certainly I will do everything I can to make that happen. And as for Katie—I know she likes and respects you because she's told me so. Besides, she wants me to be happy, and I will be if you and I are together. We'll be happy, sweetheart, we really will. And even though you say you don't believe we are meant to be happy in this world—give us a chance. You just might change your mind.

The letter remains unsigned as I rewrite it many times in pencil, trying to get the preachy parts out, but try as I will, they keep popping back in. I grip the pencil so hard a bump starts forming on my finger and after a while it hurts, so I let it be, painstakingly copy each word in ink, seal the letter, still unsigned, in the envelope. There is no name on the envelope, and the letter stays in the drawer of a bureau in a beach house closed for the winter.

SCENARIO SIX: As we are saying Good-bye, just as he's getting out of the taxi, I hand it to him—the letter, I mean. He looks surprised. Driving away, I wave, but he doesn't see this . . . he's standing in the street, reading. From the back he looks like someone else, but I can't place who. Some actor maybe? Gene Hackman . . . maybe not.

. . .

SCENARIO SEVEN: Impulsively I send the letter by overnight express to New Orleans, where he is on assignment. Bill has joined him, unexpectedly. A bellboy brings it up and hands it to her.

Just out of the shower, he calls out, "What's that?"

"Breakfast, honey," she says.

A waiter wheels in the table as she salts the letter away in her bag. "They sent up the newspaper too," she says. "Isn't that nice."

Something in her voice alerts him, but when he emerges from the bathroom nothing has changed. There she sits in her take-charge fashion, once paradoxically beguiling, now maddening beyond reason.

"Can I see you?" he says.

"What do you have in mind?" I say. (Meetings are arranged on the spur of the moment, often changed.)

"You," he says, "that's what I have in mind."

"Listen to me," I say.

"When can I see you?" he says.

Trying to keep cool, I say, "Call me later when you know what your time's like." (Variations on this dialogue go on constantly.)

But he doesn't call, and I don't hear from him again. When I do it's from a pay phone on the street. In the background there's noise—a jackhammer perhaps?

"I *must* talk to you!"

He sounds awful, but maybe it's because he's shouting.

"I'm busy; not today," I say.

"Cancel it!"

Half an hour later we meet for lunch. Over linguine at Tino's, he asks me if I've seen any good movies lately. It doesn't seem to bother him that the building he lives in with Billie is only around the corner or that we run into people we know here. On the contrary; it's as if he wants everyone to know.

SCENARIO EIGHT: He makes things so impossible for Billie she is finally the one to move out (tight-lipped but without a scene), which is what he has wanted all along.

SCENARIO NINE: They fight all the time, only my name is never mentioned. He never says no to a project, even ones he has no interest in. This is to avoid facing Billie, and his work takes on a slapdash sloppiness, which makes him more erratic and contentious than ever (his public doesn't seem to notice). He's away almost all the time, but calls me the minute he checks into a hotel. He goes crazy just hearing my voice, and we make love over the phone. This Scenario not only happens but repeats itself rather a lot. After a while there's something déjà vu about it, but neither of us is bored by this, and it goes on as before.

SCENARIO TEN: It's summer again and as usual Bill has left the hot city for the heat of Indiana, to visit her family. It's one of our many summers together (together more or less). When I return his call a woman answers—the housekeeper? But when I ask to speak to him she says, "This is Maclin's wife. Maclin's asleep. I'll take a message."

The voice is twangy, with a proprietary edge to it—a secretary

handling an unwanted business call. When he does phone it's
not because she has given him the message (which she hasn't);
it's because, he says, he doesn't know what's going to happen.
I hardly recognize his voice. We meet and make love like two
trains crashing into each other. After, he falls asleep, and as I
lie beside him, under the weight of his arm my hand goes to
sleep. But I don't move. In the half dark he looks like a
stranger—which, of course, he is.

"How do I look?" he says when he wakes up.

"Tired," I say.

"I've got to leave for Tunisia."

"No kidding."

And we both laugh.

SCENARIO ELEVEN: Bill waits for me in the street. Neither of us
has seen him for two weeks, perhaps longer. A hat is pulled
down over her wispy fringe, flattening it into her eyebrows, and
her somewhat monkey face is pinched up into her nose with
the effort of trying not to show her hatred of me. I try not to
stare at her hand resting on the shoulder strap of her bag . . .
a plain gold ring, just as I thought. What's engraved inside?
Initials and a date, no doubt. Maybe not.

"Leave him alone," she says. "He's mine!"

But already I am moving away . . .

We don't have to get married, I say.

"No," he answers, "but I would want to get married again—
it's a way of saying thank you."

Sweet, isn't it?

. . .

SCENARIO TWELVE: Same street corner, same Billie—only this time her face is scrunched up with the effort of fighting back tears. Without the hat, the face is more elfin than monkey.

"Come," I say.

And we go into Mamacita's Coffee Shop and sit facing each other. We order peanut butter waffles, which neither of us eat. They get cold in puddles of maple syrup as we drink cup after cup of coffee. The biddy-bossy voice is now a lispy croak, gargling over other girlfriends she's had to put up with—it seems I've lasted longest. She's in as much pain as I am, and I start seeing from her point of view (fatal, always). I decide to break it off and never see him again. When he calls I advise him of this, but he believes none of it and lets me dither awhile without calling. When he finally does call, I tell him I can't see him that day because I have a lunch date (with Billie actually). I now find her much more interesting than he is. She's a great listener, and I pour out to her the problems I have with my new lover, who's not married.

The phone starts to ring . . . but this time I let it. I'm not going to see him again, no, I'm not, and as the days pass I think of him less and less. It's been weeks now since even one Scenario forced itself into my burnt-up brain. Each hour that passes has a way of blurring him, and as he fades further and further into landscape, my image of him changes. I now view him as someone I invented; I too, a fantasy that fitted quite irrevocably into that fragmented logic of his. Yes, inevitable— on his part as well as mine.

. . .

SCENARIO THIRTEEN: We live in an apartment, but not their duplex. Billie got that as part of the separation. Mac got his dog Boon (for boon companion), so he resides with us. He's an old dog and mean. Billie and Boon used to get into scraps, having at each other over every little this and that, but as Mac says, "Boon hates everybody because he hates himself," so it's no reflection on Billie. I can tell you Boon's no picnic, but I put up with him cheerily, tempt him with treats, a soft toy to chew on, a bit of cheese. So far nothing woos him. I would have thought, now that Mac and I live together, that a sense of permanence would surround us. However, his work takes him away as much as it ever did, so it almost seems as if I saw more of him when he was married to Billie. And (I'd only tell *you* this) he is moody, very. Difficult. Erratic at times, *always* hard to please (God knows I try), and to tell the truth it was a lot more fun when we caught our times together on the wing, as they say, and more and more frequently I find myself looking back on the old days with a twinge of longing. But they pass, these momentary lapses, for when he is away it's in *our* closet his clothes hang. And that makes a difference.

SCENARIO FOURTEEN: Mr. and Mrs. Maclin Hollis! Our life together is even more rapturous than it was in those furtive years before we were married. Not only that—our children adore each other, with much visiting back and forth and summers at the beach house. As for Mac's travels, they occur much less often (he keeps getting better and better, you'll be glad to hear), and when they do, I of course accompany him. As for the enigmatic allergies he used to get, not to mention the unaccountable migraines (his and mine)—gone completely!

Even Billie, with time, has come to see how much happier the new situation is for all concerned, how much more suited Mac and I are to each other than ever the two of them were. It's not for me to say, but perhaps the fact that there's a new person in her life has made this inevitable happen even sooner than I always knew it would. She confided about him over lunch the other day, and he sounds perfect even if he is married. But, capable as always, she says she has the situation well in hand, and who knows what will develop? She finds it perverse that Mac has changed so completely, that it's possible to actually schedule things ahead as far as home life is concerned; to, yes, invite friends to dinner, return their invitations, spend evenings at the theater (planned well in advance), not to mention holidays in one heavenly place or another. Only last week it was Bermuda, a pink cottage on Mangrove Bay, days loafing around on one beach or another. And oooo! the nights. It just proves that you can get what you wish for and still be happy all the time.

After graduating from Radcliffe I got a job doing research for an obsessed scholar who was compiling an encyclopedia on the lions of Venice. Venetians are engagingly eccentric about lions and the city crawls with all manner of fantasy beasts, winged and otherwise, which grace every facade, garden, crest, tomb, flag, and insurance plaque. There are seventy-five lions on the Porta della Carta, the main entrance to the Doges' Palace, and I know each one as an intimate, along with every other lion in the city.

When I came back to New York I was in my thirties, Abe

ten years older, and although we'd met years before he was an acquaintance I'd forgotten. The day after I arrived, I was walking on Madison Avenue and someone said my name and turning around I saw a tall man who apparently knew me. "Abe Weatherbee," he said, seeing my bewilderment. And so it was! How nice to see him again, and as we stood there in the sunlight, I looked up into his eyes thinking how handsome he'd become, quite the most attractive man I'd ever met, married, of course— but he wasn't! "Come around to the gallery for a minute," he said. "It's just around the corner. My father died several years ago, and I'm doing the best I can to fill his place." Modest indeed, I thought later, after I'd seen what he'd made of the gallery, for he not only was a businessman as his father before him had been, he brought to the necessary shrewdness the spirit of the artist. It's funny, but I knew right away, the minute I heard him say "Jessica," that we were going to be important to each other. Oh, I did love him. And he . . . well, he always put me first.

Mac takes me to an inn near Garrison. The fall foliage is *à point*, as Claude Lubin would say. We walk in the woods, make love, and over dinner talk about movies we've seen (but not together). His attention span is erratic at best, and he walks out on most of them, so the conversation is jumpy as we go from one to another, quickly running out of movies to talk about. What's the gossip? he says. He dotes on banalities, so I make up some to amuse him.

We laugh a lot and then go to bed and make love again. But after a few days I feel oddly depleted. I've been careful not to mention Billie, because he says it depresses him. Yes, he has an endearing spontaneity, not unlike that of a rash two-year-old, but as we drive back to the city I'm wondering what it would be like if we did live together. He hasn't time to read novels or go to galleries and museums. After movies and the news, what would we talk about?

There's a lot on my mind with the business of running the Weatherbee Galleries. Still I make an effort to seriously consider Claude. How faithful has been his unspoken love for me over the years—perhaps this is the time to give it a chance, just what's needed to make the break from Mac. The timing from Claude's point of view is fortuitous as well, for he has just broken up with a girlfriend, so we have dinner and after he has gone over the whole sorry tale with me we end up in bed. It's fun but it's not Mac.

Two days after this my phone rings. I know it's him because I still haven't given that number to anyone else. I let it ring twice before picking it up. It's a wrong number. Banging the phone down, I forget about it, but later, as I loll in the bathtub, he drifts into my mind . . . how he always chooses the right side of the bed to sleep on, things like that.

Just as I'm on my way out to meet Claude, the phone starts ringing. I'm not going to answer, so why do I pick up on the third ring?

"Do you miss me?" he says.

As if nothing has changed, we start seeing each other. As if our being apart was only the usual brief separation due to one of his trips, to Moscow perhaps, with its frustrating phone connections. He and Billie are having their usual squabbles, miserable as ever, and he says sooner or later he's going to leave. The scenarios play much as they did before, only now they tend to repeat themselves. There's something draining about this, and I make up my mind that the next time I see him it really will be Good-bye, although he's not to be aware of this (you know how he hates confrontations). To do this successfully I have to really mean it. And I do.

My friends congratulate me. Felice especially. It's been wearing on her—all those duffels packed for trips that only sometimes took place. It's been a strain on Ken and Molly too. Yes, the patience of my network of friends was stretched to the limits, but they stood by me steadfast and true, supportive at every new development, never failing with their time and energy, whether to bolster sinking hopes or to rejoice with me as the pendulum swung toward the little triumphs I have had here and there in my life with Mac. They never did like him—not that they knew him except through hearsay, but still, they do seem to have an amazing grip on what he's really like and feel as I do that I've made the right decision. No more tedious calls back and forth, going over the minutiae of these ups and downs. Yes, it's a relief all around.

Still . . . recently I've started thinking about him again, the way I used to before the Good-bye. Of course, although this Good-bye has been acted upon he doesn't know it yet. The last time we parted, there were the usual wavings, ardent looks and so on, nothing to portend change. But I don't answer my phone, and when he calls the Weatherbee Galleries they advise him I'm out of town on business. After a while he'll get the message and stop calling. Ah yes! how seductive it is to be busy busy, and as the days slither by, Bill will take command again and after a while he'll forget about me as I've forgotten about him.

So why is it I've taken to calling Ken and Molly—Felice too—just to talk about him? Not only that; when I'm out of an evening (even though I'm with Claude) I find myself maneuvering him into the conversation . . . Just to have my lips shape his name lets me breathe again.

Maybe I've been hasty. It wasn't said, was it? That Good-bye. So as far as he's concerned, everything's exactly the same. But is it? As these things preoccupy me, the phone rings.

"Hello?"

Billie

"What the hell are you getting at? Come to the point—"

"Billie, I'm only telling you because I'd want you to do the same for me. It wasn't just anybody!"

"Maclin has lots of friends, lots of women he works with—"

I was alone in the apartment, talking on the phone to that stupid Patsy Plunkett, and I got all jumped up as on and on she went telling me Maclin had his arms around some woman and whoever she was kept looking up at him—get this— "radiant as a bride." I wanted to put my hand right through the phone and poke her eye out but instead said, sweet as pie, "Aside from looking radiant as a bride, how else did she look?"

"Blond, elegant. Tallish. I couldn't be really sure: in bare feet probably shorter than he is. She was wearing a pea jacket, navy—no, it may have been black—anyway a pea jacket over a swirling skirt, boots, Arpel's I think, and a black scarf blowing about and her hair windblown in a most attractive way, quite effective, I have to admit."

" 'Windblown in a most attractive way,' " I said.

"Yes, great hair—you know, that bouncy thick kind," Patsy said matter-of-factly.

"Oh, it's that what's-her-name—his new writer," I started to say, but she cut me off with: "Not from where I sat, Billie. They walked right past the taxi I was in, but don't worry, they didn't see me—much too preoccupied with each other. I'm doing you a favor, believe me, by telling you."

"Well, you can shove it," I yelled at her . . . only I didn't. Damned if I'll give her that satisfaction.

"Yes, I'm glad you told me," I said reasonably, "but it's all straight now, isn't it, Patsy poo . . . Let's get together soon— how about next Tuesday, lunch? So much to catch up on."

When she said O.K. she sounded kind of flat but not flat down enough to suit me. Of course I'm much too busy to waste time with her for lunch or anything else. I'll have my secretary call later to tell her I have to go out of town on business.

I thought over what she'd said and called sister Lurline in Evansville, but it was Saturday, her day at Sue-Ann's Beauty Emporium, and she must've not gotten home yet 'cause there was no answer and I got all jumped up again and then real mad at myself for it. Jenny was at the movies and that damn old Boon was fussing around to be taken out. You wouldn't believe what I have to put up with. He really hates me, that dog, but I have my little ways of dealing with him, just like I have my little ways of dealing with Maclin. You should see them some-times, Boon spread out fat as a hippo on Maclin's lap, the two of them glued to the television watching the football game. Then when the game's over, up Boon trots, snorting and fart-ing along after Maclin down the hall to their room, wagging his tail, pleased as punch ever since Maclin and I started hav-ing separate rooms. Tall and elegant, is she? It couldn't be her, could it? That one he's kept going back to. "Radiant as a bride . . . " Son-of-a-bitch, we'll see about that.

Jess

I dream that I meet Mac in Paris. We go to a brothel. He's been there before but alone, without me. It's in a house in the Seventeenth Arrondissement. From the outside it looks cared for, a house where rich people live, the gray stone of centuries covered with vines. The door is oak with iron motifs, and next to it, attached to the vine-covered wall, there is a bell with a chain hanging from it and a bronze figure of a monk holding a hammer, and when Mac pulls the chain the figure moves forward to strike the bell, back and forth, pong-ping. The door is opened by a woman in a long black dress with a high neck and long sleeves, a simple dress, silk jersey. She wears no jewelry, but her maquillage is done with great attention to detail. A speckling of silvery fairy dust around her eyes catches the light from the candle she is holding as she turns toward Mac.

"Bonsoir, Monsieur . . . Madame," she says, without turning toward me. Her eyes are yellow as a cat's, her mouth the color of burnt sugar. *"Marielle vous attend."*

We follow her across the marble hallway, up the curving marble steps, past balustrades of iron arabesques on either side.

"There are others waiting—in the event Marielle does not please Madame."

She turns to me as she says this and nods. We continue along passageways, past doors leading into rooms we do not enter. At the end of a long gallery, as we approach, a door opens silently. We enter a drawing room, which is large, uncarpeted. There is a scented waxy smell—verbena mixed with oil of roses?—which may come from the burnished Versailles parquet of the floor. The chairs and sofa are large, inviting, covered with white sheets of muslin tied together by strips of muslin to give a semblance of permanence. There are garden flowers on the tables, delphiniums, blue, and night-scented stock, white, and white candles lit in tall rococo silver candelabra. The French windows open to the garden, and in the summer night the curtains billow toward us, parachutes to catch the wind: the chandeliers are for an instant snow crystals, icicles falling one against the other. A candle goes out, but it is of no matter. Far away at the end of the room there is a bed, half screened by frescoed panels depicting Japanese maidens and their inamoratas. From the ceiling, with its moldings of fruit and flowers, an opaline crown is suspended, and floating from this, billows of filmy gauze cascade over the bed and down onto the floor. The walls are lacquered palest peach, the moldings paler still, in cream.

Another door opens suddenly and a girl enters. She is barefooted and wears a robe of gossamer, which drifts around her as she moves toward us, a mauve ribbon looped loosely around her waist. She is naked except for this and I am startled, for she resembles me.

"You are pleased, Madame?"

I turn to Mac to watch his face as he looks at her, but find instead that he is looking at me.

When we get into a taxi together, Mac always likes me to tell the driver our destination.

Stretched out on the bed in a hotel, if we're watching television and there's no remote control, he'll wave his hand, indicating he wants the channel changed, and since his attention span is short (unless he's watching football), there's rather a lot of getting up and going over to switch stations. Contrary to what one might think, I enjoy doing this small task.

We go to a restaurant on a Sunday and when Mac asks for the menu we are told it is buffet that evening.

"Oh, I don't like buffet," he says. "That's for a Hilton in Fort Lauderdale."

But there's no recourse except to fill our plates by going up and helping ourselves. Mac takes such a small portion that I ask him later if he wants seconds.

"Yes, but I don't want to get up again."

So I offer to do this for him and happily leave him seated at the table while I stand in line at the buffet waiting my turn to select morsels that might please him.

These three examples show how gently involved I am becoming in the scheme of things.

Billie

The way I let Patsy Plunkett get to me really riles me. Bitch— she made that call 'cause she's just plain jealous. She's had her eye on Maclin for some time—so what else is new? Well, lots of luck, Patsy—you're not his type at all, and I know just how to handle Maclin. I still get a chuckle over that time when the twins and I were with the family in Evansville and he was carrying on with that reporter on *Women's Wear*. Come July, and in he trots for his dental checkup, only to hear that the bill hadn't been paid in quite a while and it's always paid so prompt blah blah blah. Paid prompt—yes, because I write the checks. But that time I'd planned a little surprise for him and let it slip. Of course Maclin paid pronto, as I knew he would, but his check bounced higher than a rubber ball 'cause I'd transferred everything from that account to another. Lots of egg on his face but necessary as a friendly reminder that I'm in charge of his business affairs even if he's managing other ones! Bet he sometimes wonders why he ever encouraged me to take over. It pleases me to tell everyone that Maclin Hollis was my first client! They think it's real cute. Yes, I started out as just a housewife managing our budget, wouldn't have believed it if I could have seen into the future—that someday I'd be in business for myself in an office decorated by Mark Hampton, with clients beating on my door. They only try to get Swifty Lazar if they can't get Billie Elroy-Hollis. Folks in our family used to think Maryruth was the smart one, but that's 'cause she was firstborn and took charge when Momma wasn't herself. I always knew I could have done it better, knew that she was more busybody than smart, and now I've proved it. Why make myself sick over this one or that one or bring to mind times when Maclin would come home from one of his trips and I could smell her on him, whoever she was, like he'd been eating cotton candy? Mark and Tim were little then and there we'd be, the three of us, waiting, with him hooting in as if nothing had changed only it had because his wanting me was over and no matter what I did I couldn't get that lusting back. We went on for years that way but I bided my time, knowing he'd put up with anything to avoid a scene. So I used that, held on to it, occupying myself with keeping everything afloat if you know what I mean, which took my mind off whoever was with him, for they were together whenever they could be, I just knew. He'd come back preoccupied—with her, I was sure of it. Still, it would wear itself out, I thought, it always did, and I held tight. Then one night, he'd been back quite a while from one of his trips and I was asleep, but having some silly dream or other, you know how it is, and in this dream a tiger jumped on top of me and I was screaming and calling out Help! Help! But then the tiger turned into Maclin and I woke triumphant, believing he'd come back to me, because in the morning even though he wasn't in my bed I knew he had been. But later I came to know his being there had nothing to do with me, it had to do with the longing for her and my heart turned hard against him, and I was right for it never happened again and instead of a beginning it was the end. But so what? Lovemaking wasn't so hot anyway—I never did understand all the hoopla over it and I'd say that out loud to myself thinking that would make a difference and it did, it helped. Besides, there were other things to consider, more important things. Mrs. Maclin Hollis kind of things. Who would I have been if I wasn't? Well, probably I'd have gone back to Evansville—there's a lot to be said for living in a place where everybody knows your name, knows who you are, and even after all those years I really missed my folks, living far away as I did. Still it'd have been shameful going back a divorced woman. They all thought of me in New York living such a glamorous life, with famous friends and parties to go to. And go I did, but most of the time I went to those parties alone, unescorted, making last-minute excuses because even when Maclin wasn't on the road, he'd refuse to go with me, though it was him, the celebrity TV reporter, they wanted. You have no idea how he is about people, how un-friendly, how hard it was to get a toehold in New York on account of his attitude. He's like that about work too. No one who'd just met Maclin would believe this, they'd think I was making it up, 'cause he can sure charm crows off fences when he wants something. It makes me laugh to see him manipulating those big shots, putting them at ease, off guard, saying things on the TV they'll regret later. My victims, he calls them, as into battle he goes with his trusty camera crew, sure to win because he's the Master Manipulator. He always aimed to be the greatest in his field and he's more than made it. So it's bang bang—one down and that's the end of that one and on to the next. But what tickles me more than anything is that the joke's on him—the manipulator turns out to be the manipulated, the victimizer the victim: *my* victim. He's wanted a divorce for years, but all he really cares about is his work and it's easier for him to let things slide on as they are so he can concentrate on Number One, and even though I've made it on my own as Billie Elroy-Hollis, and have my own Numero Uno to think about, why shouldn't I have both? It suits me fine to keep on being Mrs. Maclin Hollis—Lord knows I've earned it! As for the others . . . they come and go, but I'll go on forever, because after that night with the silly tiger I found out I was preg—so I really had him, just like I did when I got him to marry me, telling him I was. Only this time it was different because I really was, with Jenny, and when she was born I knew he'd never leave, so what did the rest matter?

Jess

The afternoon Abe died, I sat in the waiting room of the hospital holding the hand of a woman I didn't know. Her husband too had been rushed into an operating room suddenly.

I pretended it wasn't happening by gripping her hand, eyes closed, sealing myself against the pain ripping through me and lying to myself, telling myself that I was back at the beach the summer we were so happy together. The summer Katie was six. That, and the woman's hand, were the only *real* things. Later, after Abe died, I wanted to find her, talk to her. Maybe her husband didn't die. Maybe they're together somewhere and everything is all right.

After it happened I went home to wake Katie to tell her. It was 2 a.m. and the corridors of the hospital were silent, suspended . . . waiting for something to happen. But it already had happened—my mother when I was six, my father when I was an infant. And now . . . Abe.

I was numb for a long time. So long I forget how long. I kept believing he was away on a trip somewhere and that any moment he'd walk in the door. Night would come and I'd say: It's been long enough now, Abe, come back. Daybreak and my first thought: Today. It was somewhere in that time I met Grafton Davis: the jab of a pin on a paralyzed body. Do you feel it or not? Even if you do you've no idea what part of your body it touched. But somewhere, I guess, because after we'd stopped seeing each other I'd glimpse him in this or that place, not sure if it was Grafton or just someone who resembled him. One time in Amagansett, as I drove through the village, I saw him (maybe not) with a girl, on bicycles—side by side they pedaled, her masses of hair captured in a loose braid that grazed her lovely rump as it moved on the seat, back and forth, up and down, with tantalizing grace. He said something to her and she turned her head toward me slightly, so did he, but then on they went, to become two dots in the distance.

. . .

Where was Mac that day? Close by or far away, each of us unaware of the other's existence.

I used to look down at my hands, cupping my fingers toward me, examining my nails. I'd found this stuff to put on them. It was in a bottle to apply with a wand, oh, so delicately, and it made them grow. It really did. Of course when I started seeing Grafton I stopped using it. Long nails give you a whole other point of view about yourself, don't they? and that didn't fit in with Grafton's point of view at all. How short my nails were then, blunt, unvarnished, not even buffed. I would study those nails of a stranger, on hands not mine. It took my mind off other things . . . Abe, that maybe he wasn't coming back.

It was when Katie went for her annual visit to the Weatherbees in Blue Hill that Grafton came up with the idea that I dress up in men's clothes—you know, Vita Sackville-West as a tall thin "Julian" on her jaunts to Paris with Violet Trefusis, along those lines, only Grafton was a man, of course, not another woman. No, that wouldn't have been of interest, but the way Grafton presented it quite captivated me. I'd been told my father had hoped for a boy, and according to my mother he'd "taken it rather well" when it turned out to be me. I'd often wondered what it would be like to be a boy. It was around the time Grafton brought this up that I started remembering what it was like to feel something, some sensation. If that happens, it means you're alive, doesn't it? Yes, timing is everything, and along came Grafton to pull me off into those wacky wonderful weeks—wicky-wacky, you might say; yes, definitely on the wicky-wacky side.

That first weekend in Tuxedo Park visiting his Aunt Sookie, who only started to suspect Sunday as we were leaving that maybe I wasn't his old college roommate after all. Then later the East Village and the gay bar where we won a trophy for the Best Tango Couple. Discarded later, along with other *souvenirs tendres*—pressed roses, billets-doux delivered at unexpected moments—you know, the usual flotsam and jetsam that accumulate when one is smitten. Come to think of it, there's a chill in the air today, and soon, from the mothballs, out will come the long black scarf he gave me. How he enjoyed tying me up to the bedpost, tenderly circling my waist with its itchy softness as I pleaded with him to pull it just a wee bit tighter. But sensitive lover that he was, he had an uncanny way of knowing when to stop. Ah yes! That was at the beginning, when the world lay before us like a land of dreams . . . Anyway, it's a great scarf, with a scratchiness that niggles gently at the skin before nestling comfortably on the neck. Actually, this one's the second. The first was stolen during intermission at the theater soon after he gave it to me, but next day, along with the red roses he always sent, there! through the cellophane, one just like it twined around the long stems. What a tingle as I untangled it from the prickly thorns.

Yes, everything about Grafton was impressive. That's one of the reasons I always took such care putting myself together for our rendezvous. It's time-consuming, all that—very! but even more so under the circumstances. Everything had to be just right—authentic, believable, you know. We didn't want curious looks, attracting attention, that sort of thing, and this took ingenuity: make-up tricky—very; long hair a major problem (poofed the Greek sailor's cap he so fancied way out of whack). Of course that was before Kenneth gave me one of those Italian cuts. Shorter, shorter! I egged him on as he snipped away, too impetuous almost, but we emerged triumphant with just the sort of look I knew Grafton would be keen on, a merry mix of *copain* and waif, most appealing. I'd lost weight during that time, a lot of weight, you know how it is, your breasts lose first, so I was thin, very thin, no chest to speak of. When you come right down to it, the only problem, if it could be called that, was that I looked almost too young—more like Grafton's younger brother than a buddy buddy to have fun with. But it's all in one's attitude really, and every moment in front of the full-length mirror was put to good use. While part of me would be selecting or discarding this or that vest or tie, another part worked feverishly on one improvisational situation or another . . . and I'd be *willing* myself taller, more prepossessing, less like the impostor that I was. Presto! there I'd be, a fella all revved up to meet another fella for a night on the town.

And what nights! but always starting out traditionally, with dinner at some restaurant or other. Grafton insisted on the best and he always made the reservation for nine. Just thinking about it made my heart go pitter-pat, pitter-pat. Yes, throughout the day I'd go pitter-pattering about my business here and there; at least I think that's what I did. By eight o'clock I'd be a nervous wreck, but he was always prompt and there I'd be waiting to open the door, knowing that with one blink he'd take in every detail of my efforts, and except for that last night (the fatal O. night), I never failed to enchant him. But that night there was a definite scowl as he noted the heels on boots I'd acquired for our jaunt to the Russian Tea Room. Displeased, I can tell you! Well, maybe they were a trifle too high—stretched credibility.

I'd have to pay dearly for that later (it's probably why I'd acquired them in the first place). No matter—that was the night
it happened . . .

Grafton always had romances percolating along in one place or
another, with his own rules about such things, but alas, there
are no romantic tales of two cities for Grafton, the pragmatist.
He'd comment on himself with a breezy "not fickle, not fickle,"
meaning not so to a girl called O., when he was in London,
and not so to another O., when he lived in New York, but
now he *was* unfaithful to her, so the "not fickle, not fickle"
apparently applied to me. He's much too selfish to bother fibbing
about anything, so I was impressed when, the day after we met,
he left the O. here and moved to the Volney, into one of those
rooms with a four-poster bed, so desirable for our purposes.
There were scenes, no doubt, with O. about this change, but
I dared not question him (although I thought about it a lot).
Anyway, it was the night of the unfortunate boots, which went
with some sort of Cossack outfit I'd conjured up to please him,
that we ran into her. He was right about those boots, though;
they made me look too girly, from the back especially. Of
course, noticing his displeasure, I suggested changing into another pair, which had served me well on other occasions, but
he said, "N-no. Leave them on," and out we sallied into the
rainy night.

"Do you consider yourself optimist or pessimist?" he asked.
We were standing looking for a taxi.

"Umm . . . ," I said, mysterious.

"I'm optimist," he said. It sounded important. But it was no
news to me, and just as we were about to pursue these weighty
matters further a taxi stopped in front of us. As the person

inside was getting out, a couple from across the street came dashing over to stake a claim and Grafton moved to beat them to it. Instead, suddenly he pulled me down a side street, around a corner, straight into a line of people hurrying onto a bus, and up we went along with them as the doors banged shut.

"What's up?" I said.

"Nothing, nothing." He looked out at the rain slashing against the window.

Desperately I tried to recapture the face I'd glimpsed fleetingly. All I could grasp, however, was someone under a mound of woolly hat and a military kind of coat. Forget it! She really was none of my business, and to get too curious over the ins and outs of her hold on Grafton took away from the lark of the moment. For lark it was, wasn't it?

But at the Russian Tea Room I found myself pressing on relentlessly, despite knowing he wanted to settle into serious perusal of the menu.

"Did she see us?" I persisted.

Wearily he leaned back, sulkily sipping his second gimlet. How adorable he looked! He's most partial to gimlets, made with rum, not gin or vodka. Lately I'd become more and more preoccupied with the minutiae of all things pertaining to his person. The tousle of hair, a tendril baby-fine as it crosses his brow, his slightest whim weighted with signs and portents. It was exhausting, I can tell you. I'd sensed a shift in mood and it made me uneasy, very. After all, I wasn't really a boy, was I? A *copain* to dally with, not even a girl. A woman. Panicked, I looked into the mirror behind us and that's what I saw—a woman, a woman who looked like a boy, a boy who was me.

"What would please you, darling?" he asked. "Blini with caviar, ratatouille first?"

A third gimlet was cheering him up, and he took my hand,

placing it proprietarily under the table between his legs. I pulled away, resorting to a flirty habit I have of brushing my hair back over my shoulder, but there was nothing to brush back, and the void took me by surprise.

"How long do you think we'd last under different circumstances?" I said. But this turn of conversation annoyed him, as I knew it would.

"Oh, I don't know." He waved his cigarette in the air peevishly. "We'll run into each other someplace and make love, I suppose. No doubt when you're eighty, quite by chance, and it'll happen again."

"Good Lord! Eighty."

For our next meeting I answered the door wearing spiky heels and a nightgowny something or other. I'd been at Bloomingdale's all afternoon, at the Revlon cosmetic counter, having my face made up like a custard pie. They do it free of charge, but you end up coming home with a shopping bag full of Cheeky blush-on, coordinating thises and thats, the obligatories for future maintenance. Oh well, it was worth it; we never did get to the restaurant.

After that, I drifted into letting my hair grow again, nails too, and we settled more or less into plans for summer. A rented house on the beach perhaps, or country weekends visiting friends, with a quick trip in between to Venice, or, best of all, stay on in New York (when the fools leave): side by side, his arm around me, we'd venture forth at dusk and discover the city, so various, so beautiful, so new, and so on.

Then . . .

On the phone in the middle of a conversation about a plan to go to London (his idea):

"I'll call you right back," he said.

But what of London O.? Maybe he'd left her too? Or was going to? This got me brooding, hoping he had, hoping he hadn't. If he hadn't, it might be just as well. Still I worked myself up into a dither as the days went by, yes, days and days without hearing from him. I kept calling the Volney, but—no answer. Dared I phone his mother, whom I hadn't met but who I knew resided in the Mary Manning Walsh nursing home? Surely *she* would know his whereabouts. No, such a call might confuse her. Then one day the response at the Volney wasn't "No answer," it was "Checked out," gone to London with no forwarding address. So it wasn't the London O. he left, it was me.

Right after that I found out her name. She's an actress, blond like me, and has that lace-curtain-brat look Grafton's so partial to, combined with something else you can't quite catch.

"Oh, they've been together for years," my informant said cheerily. "She was the one encouraged him to lose all that weight, exercise programs, some sort of meditation mixed up in it somewhere, you know, chants and things."

Grafton, fat? Try as I would, I couldn't picture a fat Grafton. London O. too, not at all what I pictured. I'd thought of her as an Opal or Onella, with its flavor of possible goings-on in Budapest, et cetera, et cetera; and the New York O. as bearing one of those "virtue" names so popular in early New England— Obedience, for example. Of course knowing who London O. was changed everything: Jane Esmond.

Grafton drifts in and out of people's lives, so why should I have been the exception? It is his choice to have no home, so why dwell on happily ever after? Grafton certainly doesn't, and neither did I. But it was only after he'd gone that I recognized what drew me to him: sensation. Better a body bruised than numb as it was after Abe died; no question of choice even, so why transform it into something other than what it was? But loss, even of such a minor nature, apparently unhinges my reason, for I found myself missing him and drifting in and out of that magic word forever, which has the power to turn even a frog into a prince.

With time will Mac become a hieroglyphic on the wall of a cavern somewhere in memory? Faded, so that as my finger traces over the symbols they will come to me oddly, for the name I trace is: Mother. And Grafton I'll find not at all . . . Was he but a substitute to fill the need until the more substantial representative appeared?

Jane

LONDON

Watching myself on the telly, I judge Jane Esmond and her performances objectively. Oh, come on, you might say, but it's always been that way. Even as a child I'd be playacting, referring to myself somewhat affectionately as Jelly-Jane, because she's the one I put my faith in. So I'll look at the screen, observing— she's doing that, look what Jelly-Jane's doing now—and in a play after a performance, before going to sleep, I'll run scenes inside my head, wondering why she didn't get a bigger laugh there, noting she should have turned sooner on the line about the fruitcake—but that third act wasn't bad, Jane Esmond bit into that last scene with just the right amount of fuck-you attitude the audience needs to make them sit up and take notice, which is why she got such a big hand.

After Grafton left last time, I sank into the usual doom and gloom, not over him but over the play—what a flop, and I started agonizing per usual about work. Would another part ever come along, and even if it did wouldn't Maggie Smith get it? If only I could talk myself into the same attitude about work that I have about him. Anyhow, after the play flopped, there I was in the pits when it happened, what every actress would kill for—a vehicle. Spooky, everyone said so, as if it had been created just for me. All I have to do is be myself, whoever that is, and it's not going to end the way a play or film does, a series can run on and on for years if it's a hit. So in the middle of all this Grafton surfaces again, calling to say he's flying back to London tomorrow. I almost wish he wasn't. It's only going to complicate things . . . Still it's been ages since I got a good spanking.

Always after he leaves, as the days go by the bruises on my body fade, but this makes me miss him more instead of less. I keep thinking about him, remembering how we'd be sitting in some pub over drinks and he'd inquire solicitously, inquisitively about my bottom, concerned that perhaps he'd got too carried away the night before. I get hot now just thinking about it, how I'd winced with pleasure as I sat there, cushioned seat luckily, wanting more than anything to be back in our digs just the two of us instead of somewhere with people around and plans to meet others after the theatre. When he disappears I torment myself wondering who he's with, what she's like, the girl he's with when he's wherever he is, knowing that what he gave me he's now giving her. But he'll come back, he always has—to me and to Garnet.

Garnet

NEW YORK CITY

Each time I go back to Grafton I slip into a place without memory of how or why. This annoys me about myself, because each time we part it's only a matter of time before we're back together again, and there's Jane, as always, waiting in the wings to make her presence known in the usual ways, or else it is I who wait, although I'm not aware of what I'm waiting for until later, when the three of us are together again.

It all goes back, of course, to that first time a hundred years ago in New York when Grafton met some woman and moved out to be with her. I was used to his leaving me for the one in London, but not *this*. No—I wouldn't put up with one of his attachments in *our* city. Then months later he called, insisting I meet him within the hour. Of course I said I wouldn't, that I never wanted to see him again. But he said it was important.

"Important to you or important to me?" I said.

"Garnet, I'm leaving *tomorrow*."

So I said, "O.K. I will."

And I did.

It wasn't the Volney, where he'd gone when he moved out of our place so he'd be free to see the New York girl he'd taken up with; it was another hotel.

"Why the Saint Regis?" I asked.

"A special occasion—you'll see."

And there he was already waiting in the lobby when I arrived. I'd steeled myself but up until the last moment thought about not showing up, just letting him wait and wait until he'd accepted the fact that I'd left and wasn't coming back. On the way there in the taxi I kept thinking about the other one, waiting for him in London, and at the same time wondering about the one here, the one he'd left me for, curious about how she was taking it, curious to know how she was getting adjusted to Grafton's way of doing things. He was in one of his subdued moods sitting there, exhausted probably from a debauched night. Still he looked familiar, a friend of long standing, an old friend I'd known forever. And it startled me, this. Then as we went up to the room he had taken, in the elevator I started wanting him, shaking inside when he looked at me and said:

"I've missed you . . . Garnet?"

I didn't look at him or answer him, just stood there facing the doors as they slid open, then followed him on down the hall to Room 602. It was a small room, the walls hung with green taffeta. A fire had been lit. On the table in front of it there was a silver bucket with ice in it and a bottle of champagne—Cristal.

"Why did you ask me here?" I said. I was still standing, though he had stretched out on the bed.

"Come here," he said.

"No!" And I turned away, deciding I'd leave and knowing if I stayed longer I wouldn't.

"I have something to say to you," he said, "something I've been thinking about for a long time."

"I'm not interested."

But he said quickly, "Then why are you here?"

"I don't know." And I didn't.

"I wanted to ask you about something," he said, and he got off the bed and went over to the table and ceremoniously opened the bottle of champagne.

"Look, I've got to go, someone's waiting for me."

"Ah, a new romance." He smiled, filling the goblets.

"That's hardly your business, it it?"

I started to the door, but he handed me a glass, saying, "A toast before you go—a toast to you coming to live with me in London."

It took me by surprise, it really did, and he kept watching me as he went over to the bed and stretched out again.

"What about *her?*" I asked.

"What about her?" He yawned.

"Well, is it over between you, did you break it off with her long distance to London when you did with me?"

"Not that I know of," he said. "She's expecting me, and I don't think she'll mind at all having you as our guest. I think you might both enjoy it."

"And what about the other one, the one here—has she been invited too?"

He laughed and held his hand out to me. I went over to the bed and stood looking down at him.

"Let me think about it," I said.

"There's nothing to think about really, is there?"

No, there isn't—not when you love someone.

So I went, and that's how I met Jane.

Jane

LONDON

We were supposed to shoot on location in Runnymede that day but it was postponed due to rain so I was at the flat when he arrived. I heard the key in the lock and I ran to the door as it

was opening and there he was, but with someone—a woman—
and he said, "Jane, this is Garnet, Garnet Blackburn."

And luggage, more than the usual luggage, his and her luggage, was plunked right behind them in the hall by the lift.
She stood there smooth as cream, her hand out, expecting me
to move forward. Reserved, I'd call it, her manner, none of
that pushiness the Americans have, quite formal, saying,
"Hello. I've been looking forward to meeting you. Grafton's
told me so much about you."

"Indeed?" I said.

"Yes," she answered simply.

Her speech too was different from the usual American, softer.
Maybe she's Latin or something, I thought. There's a look about
her—dark Irish maybe? What kind of a name is Garnet anyway?
Grafton was going back and forth lugging suitcases into the flat,
filling me in on future plans. It seemed she'd be staying with
us for a while, sleep on the couch in his studio and so forth.

"What about your paints and things?" The question came
out edgy, sarcastic.

"Oh, it'll work out fine," he shouted from the hall, while
Her Serene Highness stood there and a mouse started whizzing
round and round inside my head, trying to get out. I looked
into the tall mirror by the door, where we were both reflected,
she and I. We were the same height, exactly. How sleek her
fringe of bangs, the straight hair curving crisply into a helmet
of dark sable, the skin translucent and the face with its trace
of the *enfant gâté* so contradictory to the energy of her body,
slim and arrow taut, about to shoot into Grafton. And next to
her—Jelly-Jane with honeybun breasts and yellow ringlets, quite
the cartoon, her kittycat eyes taking it all in, not just Garnet
but the hall and the white-hot room behind as a shadow appeared in the frame and now there were three and Grafton was

looking straight past Garnet, looking at Jelly-Jane as if Garnet didn't exist, as if he'd come back alone, back home to me.

Garnet

There's a white hammock at one end of the studio strung across a beam in the high ceiling. Grafton used it for a commercial illustration and after the model finished posing he left it there. It's inviting despite the awkwardness of settling oneself in, and I use it sometimes to float suspended, turning my body loose in this white world, swaying gently, becoming white and spare as this enormous room. Below me a white sea and above, the ceiling—a white sky—and on the white walls Grafton's paintings, haphazard spatterings, white on white, fading into the white canvas. It's peaceful as rain pats the skylight, peaceful on other days too, when the room is soothed by the flat north light. Still I'll be leaving soon. At least I think I will. This isn't a ménage à trois. No, it never has been. I simply came here because I did. And I can leave anytime. After all, this is not my studio. That is elsewhere. In New York I have a loft of my own where my paintings hang and a gallery that sells my work and a bed that is mine. I tell myself this as I stare up at the white sky, tell myself I can choose to no longer be a cloud, drifting in and out of Grafton's life, changing shape as the wind blows. This pleases me—this decision—and I wonder why it's taken so long to come to it.

The look of the three of us in this room I quite like. Grafton appreciates it too. Perhaps that's what brings me back. Jane's always a surprise. Usually when you see an actress she partly resembles her screen persona. But Jane doesn't, even half. In a café or standing next to you in line waiting to get into a movie, I don't think you'd recognize her. With the spun-sugar ringlets in disarray around her face and her albino-white skin without make-up, she resembles one of Grafton's sketches indecisively rubbed over—what remains is the imprint of a child deprived, but with a street-smart kid lurking somewhere inside, hidden, waiting for the right moment to jump out at you. Lolling on Grafton's mattress here in this room, she is as white on white as the paintings on the walls, and as I stretch out beside her I am curious to know how he perceives me—the contrast of the blue-black Japanese hair as it falls straight around the white face. Puzzling over this I drift, letting go, floating above the white sea.

Jane

My real name isn't Jane. It's Marygold. At least it was. At the orphanage we were all just numbers, I would imagine. But even though I was a number amongst all the other numbers I was different and knew it. It was my first memory, my *very* first. Honest. I must have been two years old or so but we won't go into that because I always fib about my age whenever I know I can put one over—anyway, now of course I've come to realize that everyone else thinks this same thing about himself, we all start off with the secret feeling that we're different, so there wasn't anything special about me after all as I kept up, along with the others, breathing on hope, waiting to be discovered. Sooner or later something would happen . . .

It was odd though, because from the moment when I knew I was different, when I knew that there was a real me who had nothing to do with the one living in that dreary greyness, that real me had no name and floated around inside somewhere, out of reach. Now and again there'd be glimmers of a golden fish swimming through crystal caverns, but every time I reached down to catch her my hand plunged into tangled seaweed and came up empty.

In the beginning there were times when I wished Grafton would just leave the two of us alone, but I didn't tell him that, or Garnet either, for that matter. She has the most exquisite nose, slightly indented, molded at the tip like a petal on a flower that has no name, a flower you feel compelled to touch. I'm thinking of going to that famous surgeon on Harley Street and taking her there with me. I'll point to it and say, Give me that nose! It's all Jelly-Jane needs to make her happy in this world. You think I'm joking. I'm not. I wonder if she knows how beautiful she is. Sometimes when she looks at me I'd give anything to know what is going on in that head of hers, but she played it cool right from the first, had it all figured out. As though there was a big secret and she knew the answer. And I had to find out what it was. Once we're alone she'll tell me, I thought. But she never did and still hasn't. Most days I'll be at rehearsal or filming and she'll be around somewhere while Grafton is working in the studio. Sometimes she poses for him, but I've never been crazy for the results. He doesn't get her at all, at least not in the way I do. Maybe I don't really either. Maybe because I covet that nose of hers I keep thinking that underneath her remoteness there's someone like me, and once I find her I'll know who I am. What do they talk about all day? I get so jealous imagining maybe he's making love to her without my being there. Then I go batty and mess up a scene; not intentionally, you understand, it just happens. "Whatever you're doing, stop it!" the director will say. So I try to comply. Look, if you can't get along with Jane Esmond you can't get along with anyone. Right? Well, maybe.

Jess

NEW YORK CITY

How often Mac's said:
"The eagle flies alone."
And how it upsets me, because finally that must be what he wants (or is it?), and I start collecting irreverent thoughts so that I'll love him less. How fragmented, driven, lacking in sensitivity to anyone except himself—all these things he is. He puts everyone else *on the other side*. It has to be, I suppose— it's the anger and hostility directed at his subjects that gives him the impetus to do his work. He admires this in himself, holds on to it, nurtures it, is suspicious, loath to trust—while I trust first though later may be betrayed. Chaos he relishes. Plans made to be changed a moment later, the wily ploys, the secrets of his trade, which make him a Master Manipulator (as he says) and tops in what he does.

"There were those years, when I was getting started," he said once. "Television was an unknown quantity then, no one knew where it was going and neither did I—I just wanted to get there. Damned if I know why but those days still have a grip on me, drive me to take on too much now—afraid if I say no I'll lose everything."

"How actory," I said.

"Actory?"

"Well—no matter how successful actors are it's never enough—somewhere inside they always believe the part they're playing is their last."

And so he says yes to everything, yes to this although he's already said yes to that, juggling along—if this falls through, there'll be that to do.

Then he added, unexpectedly, "It's also wanting to be far away as often as possible from Billie. We haven't been to bed together in years—never should have gotten married." His hand went over his eyes and he pressed his fingers into his temples and took a deep breath. "I was in the army and some girls from the Evansville Junior League came to the base with a show they'd put together to cheer us up."

"And one of them was—"

He nodded. "She was sexy."

"In what way?" I asked.

"You just wanted to fuck her. All the guys wanted to, but she singled me out right away, and a few months later we were about to be sent overseas and she told me she was pregnant so I married her the day before we shipped out."

"Seems like an old story," I said.

"So—there we were."

"And here we are," I said.

"When the war was over, all I wanted to do was work, and she fitted into things, took over, made it easier for me to do what I wanted, and it was easier, too—to make the best of it. Now . . ."

He was silent for a while and then he said, "She embarrasses me."

Oh God, I thought, there's no answer to that.

Billie

Maryruth was a real pain in the ass when I started my agency. "Agency!" she hoity-toited over the phone. "Are you nuts? What about Maclin?" First of all, Maryruth, I said logically, to keep in charge of the conversation, clear your mind for just a minute and think of the opportunities that surround me, hundreds—no, thousands—of contacts I've built up over the years. Going to those parties finally paid off I can tell you. What with Jenny growing up and Mark and Tim long since on their own, I owe it to myself to take my contacts and use them instead of continuing so unselfishly to devote my time and energy exclusively to running the house. "Naturally," she said. Don't you be sarcastic with me, I told her. "You misread me, Sister-baby," she said. "You know I've only your best interests at heart—I just don't want you to mess up your fine marriage." Don't Sister-baby me, I said, and it's not *that* fine. "What's that? What did you say?" It'll be fine, Maryruth, I said, so that shut her face for the moment. But then she went right on advising me that Lurline's two girls had been taking one of those courses in home decorating and they'd be a real help with the decorating of my new office. Maryruth, how dear of you to come up with that suggestion, I told her, but I don't need my nieces to help with my decorating, or anything else. Already I've got several very important clients, I told her—stretching it a bit—not just commercial artists but—"Sounds great, Billie Mae," she said, cutting me off, "hey I've got to go now." Me too, I said, I'm already late for my first appointment, but I kept it cool and the conversation ended on a polite note. Still I was damn put out by her attitude, bossy one that she is, just 'cause she's firstborn. She always did try to lord it over me every chance she got. Well, Big Sister, it's Baby Sister's time to twinkle.

Of course I'm not really the babiest sister. Easter is. But she doesn't count anymore with us Reddys. We're all mighty successful in our chosen fields, just about as famous as she is, and I feel sorry for Easter, I really do. We have something she threw away—the security of each other and taking pride in each other's achievements. Yes, even with Maryruth's meanness, I know she boasts to people behind my back about her Baby Sister, the Late Bloomer of the family. Papa'd be real proud of us all, Elroy and Dean having carried on his chiropractor's practice, and Lurline and Amy long ago pulling out of their lazy-daisy ways and making careers in the front office, while Maryruth took charge of the accounting before Elroy and Dean franchised themselves and branched their services out to the major cities in the South and Midwest. If only Papa could see his grandsons Elroy and Dean Junior taking over the practice and following in their dads' footsteps. Not that Elroy and Dean Senior have retired. Fact is they're busier than ever, promoting the business and appearing in TV commercials—real cute ones that caught on right away and made the Reddy Twins famous everywhere they go, with folks pestering them for autographs. They're both lovable on the TV screen, and it wouldn't come as too much of a surprise if they decided to take a whack at politics. Maryruth's really pushing this idea. She says she'll never retire and is an indefatigable traveler, buzzing here and there to keep an eye on the franchises.

Sometimes I let myself look back on things and I can't help but think how sad it was that it took Papa's passing to bring Momma to her senses and that he never lived to see her come into her old self again, or all that's happened since. And that

Momma too left without knowing that Easter won the Oscar for her performance in *Nightwood*, because even though she denies us she's still Momma's child, still our kin.

My Papa was Neville James Reddy, the most respected chiropractor in Evansville, and my Momma, Virgilia Lou, née Elroy, born and raised in Louisville, Kentucky, was a real lady. We lived in a fine neighborhood with only one Catholic family on the block, in the house next to us. There were a lot of folks in town who thought the Catholics were no good—well, there was talk they were planning to set up the Pope in Washington, with a secret tunnel straight from Rome to the White House. All the Catholics in the United States, even our neighbors, were in on the plot, but Papa said they were really nice folks, just misguided, and if we kept at them they'd come around in time to a right way of thinking. That's one reason why the Klan was so important. Of course I was only itty-bitty in my crib then and didn't know until later about the whippings and lynchings and whatnot.

Naturally, Papa was a member of the Klan, which is how he and Momma came to meet David C. Stephenson personally. Known as Steve, he was famous all over the country. It was only after we got to know him real well that we Reddys started calling him Keb. That was the special name Momma gave to him. It has mystical powers, that name, 'cause it comes from the Book of the Dead, which is the original book of magic and kind of like the Bible in Egypt, I think—anyway, in this book Keb is an ancient earth god. He's pictured sometimes with a goose on his head and is called "the great cackler" 'cause he laid the egg from which the world sprang. Some cackle, eh? But Momma thought it fitted him to a tee. Keb was the Klan's most important and powerful member and had millions and millions of dollars in real estate holdings all over the country and in other businesses too. Everywhere he went, there were bodyguards around him, he had fleets of automobiles and the whole top floor of the McCurdy Hotel in Evanston, plus a huge mansion in our suburb of Irvington. Of course the women were all after him, but Keb paid no heed. He let it be known that when the time came, God would place in his path the helpmate worthy to walk by his side and until such time he would travel alone.

Once, Momma took me on the yacht, *Li'l Josephine*, Keb kept on Lake Michigan. An outing, she called it. I must have been really tiny, 'cause all I remember is sitting on Momma's lap with the hot wind stinging my face red as water sped by and a big red man sitting next to Momma, leaning too close and smelling of something awful. He kept calling Momma "Vir-gie Lou-Lou Lulu lu looooo" and tickling my toes as I sat there in her lap while they laughed and carried on. Papa didn't come with us that day, and I was frightened and wanted to go home.

Looking back on it, why they stuck by Keb when things took the turn they did is something it's hard to figure out. But right up to the day she died, deep-down Momma still worshiped Keb, even though she never wanted his name mentioned. Anyway, before any of the trouble came, it was an honor for us Reddys to be chosen for Keb's innermost sanctum. We'd been in attendance whenever he preached and glued to the radio when he gave his weekly sermon, so it was a real thrill when we made his personal acquaintance and he took a genuine liking to us. After that it was one big automobile after another whisking us away to wherever crowds were gathering to hear him. Keb'd have seats for us, right near the stage so's we'd be close by as he reached up into heaven to receive the message of Jesus.

After it was over it was hard to recall just what the message was, but you knew it was something that came right down from the sky into Keb direct from Jesus and it carried you away, who knows where, making you believe, but who knows what? Wherever or whatever, it got a hold on you, the craving to see Keb and hear him again, get that feeling again, the feeling of being good even though you knew you were bad. So maybe it was no surprise after the Klan turned on Keb Momma went right on like nothing had changed, and even though her last baby, Easter, the one she hadn't planned on, was born in January of that same year, her mind was more preoccupied with the dastardly things happening to Keb than heeding what the baby was up to.

Keb was a "prodigy," according to Momma. What's that? I asked. "A marvel, that's what! Why, he's mightier now than his Emperor General of France." She was referring to Keb's Napoleon collection, which was spread about all over his Irvington mansion, in every room of his suite on the top floor of the McCurdy Hotel in Evansville, on his yacht, *Li'l Josephine*, and on his self, every kind of Napoleonic knickknack you could think of. There were ashtrays with the Emperor's profile silhouetted on them and cuff links specially made for him in New Orleans with the same profile raised up on itty-bitty cameo miniatures; a pinkie ring too. A bust of Napoleon wearing his hat stood on his desk in the mansion, but not only there—it'd been duplicated many times and placed in prominent positions wherever Keb was. Not that Keb looked anything like the Emperor—to begin with, the Emperor was short and Keb was big and tall and had red hair. Keb was the first man I'd ever seen in real life, or ever have seen since, with that kind of soft carroty-red hair. It was real special, that hair, cheruby hair I call it, 'cause it was downy curly like the hair on those cherubs that sport around in Italian paintings. The skin on his face was soft as a peach, and on the soft-peach face, like they were pasted there, were carroty-red eyebrows to match, and they arched over the piggiest blackest eyes you ever saw, but those eyebrows were so thin they looked like they'd been plucked the way a movie star's are. His mouth was kind of loose, with a moist pouty look to it sometimes, especially when he was charming Momma, and his face was puffy too, with pudgy hands to match. This doesn't make him out so handsome, as I'm describing him, I mean, but there was something about him. He could be real sweet, I guess you could say cherubic, or real crude like some carny hawker in a circus—you just never knew with Keb which way the wind'd blow, 'cause one moment it was cold and icy in a way that gave you goose pimples and chilled your blood and made you scared though you didn't know why, or it could turn on you sweet and warm as summer breezes, making you feel blessed and good again. It was only during the trial that folks found out how he'd told untruths about things—some things, that is. Like saying he'd been born in Oklahoma instead of his true place of birth, which turned out to be Texas. But the worst of his untruth telling was about never having been married, 'cause he had been—not once but twice, and divorced too, and there'd been a third wife he'd left without divorcing or even telling her Good-bye. Momma said all these things popping out at us were only snakes let loose by evil forces and they were *lies lies lies* and all the jury had to do was look at Keb's face to see the beacon of veracity shining through from inside the depths of his very soul and they'd soon be on their knees apologizing and asking Jesus' forgiveness for having let evil thoughts take hold of them. And Keb hadn't told untruths about everything. It was true, like he said, that he'd gotten into politics after World War I by organizing veterans, which had gotten him on the ballot in the Democratic congressional primary in 1920, and it was true that he'd been a second lieutenant, but it wasn't true, like he told folks, that he'd seen service overseas, for he never set foot out of the country all during the war. True that when he'd been defeated by the Anti-Saloon League he'd become a dry Republican right away and right away after that had joined the Knights of the Ku Klux Klan and organized them so well he was one two three organizing our whole proud state of Indiana, along with twenty other states in the Midwest. It was about that time that he moved his offices to Indianapolis, which is when Papa and Momma became personally acquainted with him, and it was soon after that that they piled us all into the car to attend the tristate Klan rally in Kokomo. There, at Melfalfa Park, we witnessed Keb being made the Grand Dragon of Indiana, and even after all these years and although I wasn't much more than a baby at the time, the ecstasy of that day is something you just never get over.

Waiting in the heat of the car, creeping along the highway with hundreds of others to get to Kokomo, we near drove Momma crazy. There always was something about sister Lurline's cheeks that was made to be slapped, and finally Momma couldn't stand being crushed in the heat of that Chevy in traffic another minute and she up and gave those cheeks of Lurline's a real smackeroo. Then she had to give twin sister Amy's a slap too. They let out a big howl, and after that, even though it was still too hot to live, the sisters fell asleep and things quieted down a bit. There were two hundred thousand members on the highway that day, coming from every corner of Illinois, Ohio, and Indiana to wait in Melfalfa Park under that blazing hot sun. After we finally made it, Papa held me up so I could see above the thousands of white-sheeted figures standing all around us. There I was, cute as a button in my little white hood like the others, waiting and waiting, looking upward to the sky. Then from far away, way up in the distance came a tiny speck of light, a bitty ball of fire, and the crowd let out a roar and the roar soared up into heaven to that itty-bitty speck circling above us but coming closer and closer until, near blinding us, it landed in our midst. A big tall man in a robe of purple, with a hood of purple only half covering his mop of cheruby hair, descended from the plane and a group of dignitaries moved forward to greet the messenger of God, bowing to him as they went.

"Kigy," the messenger called out.

"Itsub," the dignitaries chanted.

Then the messenger of God turned and led the group of dignitaries through the multitudes to the steps of the platform, which was strung with flags and bunting. Up he went slowly and solemnly, up the steps onto the rostrum, where he stood scanning the multitudes who waited for him to speak. He was late, because the President of the United States had kept him, counseling upon vital matters of state. "The President!" Momma hissed up at Papa, giving him the elbow. "President Warren Gamaliel Harding!" she hissed down at Elroy and Dean, who kept picking their noses and gaping.

Keb went on and on about our uplifted land and ended by officially proclaiming that he was by virtue of God's unchanging grace now the duly attested exalted Grand Dragon of the Invisible Empire for the Realm of Indiana. Well, the crowd went hog wild, I can tell you, screaming their heads off, Momma crazy wild, Papa standing tall and proud, until finally Keb, Grand Dragon Plenipotent, raised a hand and launched into a speech, something about how we must all fight for "one-hundred-percent Americanism" against "foreign elements" that were trying to control the country. Then he stepped back from the rostrum and someone threw a coin up onto the platform. After that there was mayhem—coins, trinkets, money, rings, anything flashy and of value was hurled onto that platform, piling up around Keb as he stood with his arms reaching out to us. Momma was even going to pitch in her wedding ring— Papa tried to restrain her, not that he could have—but her finger had swelled up in the heat and it wouldn't come off, so she tore her gold beads from around her neck instead. As things died down, Keb, Grand Dragon of the Invisible Empire, motioned to his underlings to sweep up the littered treasure and made his way from the platform, down the steps, and as he did a sudden breeze blew from nowhere and the purple hood fell back onto his shoulders and his hair swirled and flamed around his head like a halo, and the crowd parted as the Red Sea parted for Moses in the Bible and he proceeded on through the multitudes toward the pavilion close by, to confer with his attendant Hydras, Great Titans, Furies, Giants, Kleagles, King Kleagles, Exalted Cyclopses and Terrors. Yes, a ball of light, that's how he came to us that day, shooting down through the blue sky from heaven. Grand Dragon of the Invisible Empire for the Realm of Indiana—David C. Stephenson—our Keb.

Right up to the end Momma held to the belief Keb'd been framed by that Oberholzer creature. Wasn't his fault, she said; he had animal magnetism and had to fight the women off. Folks were just plain jealous. As for his having nigger blood, Momma went plain wild over that when it came out the second day at the trial—Keb's birth certificate having been thrown into the proceedings first thing that day as evidence of his perjuring himself about his true origins. Well, it was some bombshell in the courtroom; folks sat there just plain flabbergasted, thinking maybe they hadn't heard right. But Momma'd heard right, all right, and she started screaming her head off, and when the judge ordered her removed from the courtroom she fainted dead away and Papa had to carry her out. Back home, she came to and carried on even worse and finally Papa had to get ol' Doc Swenson over to give her a whiff of ether. But next day there she was, up before dawn, putting on her best hat, the white straw with the cherries, and her best dress, the one with rows and rows of tiny cherries dotted around all over it, and telling Papa to hurry-up hurry-up, and before the sun had risen off they went, leaving Maryruth stuck in the house in the heat all day, looking after baby Easter. Ma was raring to go, dead set on finding a way to put an end to the vile "rumor," as she called it, which was all part of this vicious plot perpetrated by certain jealous, evil individuals who were out to get Keb. She kept wheedling at Papa to intercede for him with the Klan and Papa did all he could but they slammed the door in his face, saying that the scandal Keb had brought down on them might just about do them in, and Papa got scared they'd throw him out too, so he kept his mouth shut. But Momma wouldn't let go and drove Papa near crazy, nagging at him day and night to make the Klan take a stand and prove that all the vile things being said about Keb were plain *untrue*. Let it be, let it be, Virgie, Papa kept begging, but she wouldn't and kept on at him *lies lies lies* and he pulled back more and more into his self where she couldn't get at him. As for Madge Oberholzer—nobody'd heard of her up until then, nobody important, that is, and even after the verdict came in and everyone had turned against him there were still a handful of friendly folks who would never believe that Keb, our Grand Dragon of the Invisible Empire for the Realm of Indiana, could have been lured into sinful ways by the likes of her and who were sure it was *her* fault, not his, throwing herself at him the way she did. Why would Keb be tempted into lustful ways by a dumpy spinster woman with tight wavy curls trying to hide her big ears, not to mention the bittiest nose you ever saw, when he could have any lady he might wish the company of. If only our great President Warren Gamaliel Harding hadn't passed on, none of this would have happened . . . still Momma said Papa must go to Washington, D.C., direct to President Coolidge, and inform him about it: our President would set things straight. Yes, he would.

But of course Papa didn't go to Washington. And Momma traipsed day after day to Noblesville in the sweltering heat to sit in the courtroom, tormenting herself and dragging Papa along with her. That summer was the hottest summer on record all across Indiana since God knows when, but the crowd in that little courtroom, jammed in there day after day, ate that trial up like they were giving away ice cream. Momma'd been contented as a clam and gained forty-five pounds when she'd been preg with Easter, but that summer it started slipping away from her 'cause of the Lucky Strikes and Coca-Colas—all day long Cokes and ciggies, puff puff, one after the other and not eating enough to keep a bird alive, when she'd never smoked before, not a day in her life. Even when she wasn't preg Momma'd always tended toward the plump side, but just right. There was never a time I can remember when a compliment came my way that the person paying the compliment didn't temper it by saying, "but no one's prettier than your ma, Virgilia Lou." Now, that summer, her beauty started to disappear; it faded and faded as she got thinner and thinner. Even her golden hair faded, like leaves coated with dust, and when she wasn't carrying on she'd stand staring at Easter sleeping there in her bassinet, thinking deep Momma thoughts that none of us knew the why or wherefore of. Folks started talking, thinking she was ill, real sick, sick with the dreaded sick no one dared speak of. But she wasn't. It was just plain nerves, worrying over Keb, that did this to her, fretting and worrying about what was going to happen to him.

There'd been talk, of course, and lots of gossip about this one or that one when any lady'd been seen with Keb, but they were always beauties and it just didn't set right that Keb'd be lusting after this Madge unless it was the devil's deed working to lure him into temptation. Momma *knew* that's what it was and that Satan'd gotten a hook into Keb through Madge Ober-holzer, a hook of a sexual nature, and whatever this hook was, it near drove Momma up the wall. It brought out a side in her we'd never seen before. "Look at the creature," she would say, punching an ice pick at the pile of newspaper pictures she collected of Madge to torment herself with. "Ugly ugly ugly wumps," she'd say, having at Madge's eyes with the ice pick. The day it came out in court that Keb'd cared enough about Madge to have a bill in the legislature squashed out of existence because it would have done away with Madge Oberholzer's state job, Momma held on to herself just till she made it out of the courtroom and into the car, then she let go: "Ugly ugly wumps," she screamed out the window, pointing at a woman who was piling out of the courthouse with the rest of the crowd. This woman was holding a real cutie-pie baby in a pink bonnet and Momma kept pointing at the baby and screaming, "Baby ugly wumps," and she even tried to jump out of the car to get at that cute baby, but Papa grabbed at her in time and drove away.

All through throwing supper together she kept muttering to herself, "Baby ugly wumps," and so on. It wasn't easy, I can tell you.

"I *am* the law," Keb used to say, and now Momma started muttering this to herself—that is, when she wasn't muttering over new testimony 'bout Keb every day at the trial. Remember that! Keb *is* the law! she'd say to no one in particular. Then she'd call it out again real loud like she was reading it from the Bible. So what's there to worry about, Virgie, Papa'd mumble; the good Lord will prevail.

But the morning Madge Oberholzer was to take the stand, the Lord prevailed in a way no one expected. When her lawyer went to the rooming house where Madge lived to escort her to the courthouse he found her all dressed up to testify, but instead of being ready to go she was lying with a bottle of bichloride of mercury tablets all around her on the floor, dead.

Keb was accused of being responsible for her death, and that could mean *murder*, and after that it was not only the Klan but every last one of Keb's political friends who turned their backs on him, every last one, even when Keb was forced by their disloyalty to tell those so-called friends that if they wouldn't stand by him he'd be forced to open up his "secret coffer," which had papers in it showing proof positive of what *they'd* been up to, those "guardians of government." But woe on woe, it only backfired on Keb, and they all ended up in jail—the mayor of Indianapolis, the sheriff of Marion County, a congressman, and the governor himself—all indicted for bribery. The Klan was near done in by the goings-on. Who could ever believe again in Dragons, Exalted Cyclopses, King Kleagles, Grand Goblins, Great Titans, and Imperial Wizards, much less give them responsibility for folks' righteousness? Everyone, including Republicans and Democrats, washed their hands of them, denying they'd ever had anything to do with the Klan, and the boss of the Democrats, Frank Baker, spoke right out in the newspapers saying the Klan was a "poisonous animal that we don't want to crawl into our yard and die." The same day the papers came out, Boss Baker repeated these very words himself, on the radio, and his voice boomed right into our sitting room, with our Momma sitting there having at her ciggies and Cokes. Elroy tried switching the radio off fast before she could hear, but she was faster and snatched at his hand real fierce to stop him. So she heard every word, and after she did she ran through the house, from room to room, and on out into our yard, around and around in circles. Papa got on the phone fast as he could to Doc Swenson, saying hurry over quick, and he sure did, but when Momma spotted his car driving up she leaped right over the fence into the yard next door, mashing down Mrs. Potts's tomato plants like she was mashing potatoes. Maryruth and Elroy and Dean were all chasing after her, but she was too quick for them, running around like a chicken with its head chopped off, that was our Momma, babbling funny and hitting out at them whenever they got close, and when poor old Doc Swenson finally nabbed her she bit right into his thumb like it was a hot dog and sprinted away, clucking things like "funzy wunzy Josey phonsey chosen onesey," and then, just before Doc got the ether on her, she got calm and still as death, and she looked up into the sky and said, clear as day, "The messenger of God put Jesus in me but it was Mary Mother of God who came to me on Easter Day."

Long after the trial was over, Momma couldn't get back to herself again. She just sat all day long with her Coca-Colas and her ciggies listening to country music on the radio, near driving us all nuts with the sound turned up real loud and a dish next to her filling with butts while she waited for the letters that came from the state pen at Michigan City. Even when Keb'd served enough time with good behavior to come up for parole, even though he never set foot in our doorway again, those letters kept showing up from this place or that place. Momma

sure came to when the postman arrived, getting up out of her
chair and shuffling on fast out to meet him and then going into
her room, banging the door behind her. We knew where she
put them, those letters, in a tin trunk on top of the chifforobe,
where she kept newspaper accounts of the trial. We knew too
that the key dangling on a chain around her neck, which she
never took off, not even when she took a bath, was the key to
that tin trunk. During the trial, Maryruth'd had to take over
looking after baby Easter and the running of things, but it soon
got too much even for Big Sister and Papa asked our cousin
Della, who lived alone anyway, to move in with us and after
that things were better. Eventually the uproar over Keb died
down and we stopped thinking about it so much, until we lost
our Papa. There never were any more letters, they just stopped
coming, it seemed, when Papa died, and one day the chain
disappeared from around Momma's neck and Della went away
and Keb became someone none of us wanted ever to hear of
again.

I'd never admit to a living soul the way Momma put Easter on
the back burner, so to speak, during that time, 'cause she more
than made up for it later, after she got back to herself again.
But nothing our Momma did pleased Miss Easter or was good
enough for her. By then she knew she was prettier than most
anyone in town and real determined to use that to get anything
she wanted. Early on—too early—the men were buzzing around
her, and Momma kept pumping it into her that she was a *virgin
girl*. "You're a virgin girl," Momma'd say, but Easter would just
smile and say nothing, which drove Momma up the wall wondering and worrying. Like they say, that girl thought her ass
was made out of strawberry shortcake, and the worry of where

it might lead near killed Momma. Then one day when Momma was at her wits' end about the situation, Easter just up and left—ran away from home, God knows where or with whom. Anyway, we rallied around Momma, telling her it was the best thing could have happened and not to worry, Easter'd be fine wherever she landed, but Momma kept shaking her head as she went about her day-to-day business, taking time out to pray more than usual, not neglecting her family in any way, just withdrawing more and more into her precious self. Even after that letter from her arrived, written in thick black ink like a tarantula'd dunked his feet in his own blood and crawled across the page with thick black legs dripping its thick black blood— even after Momma'd read it, she went right on, almost like the mean evil things hadn't sunk in: that our Momma loved Lurline and Amy, Maryruth, Elroy, Dean and me more than she'd ever loved her, and that Momma'd never paid attention to her or noticed she took breath since the day she was born. It said she never wanted to see any of us again and to leave her alone and not try to find out where she'd gone or anything about her. Pages and pages of mean terrible untrue lies came in that letter—Registered—to our Momma, one year to the day after the disappearance. In those 365 days, our little Momma'd been through the valley of death, bravely waiting for news, never suspecting for one second that her baby daughter Easter, the one she loved the most, harbored all that anger and resentment over the lack of attention she had gotten from Momma, though God knows there was enough attention from the rest of us, which should have satisfied her greedy self and more than made up for the time of the trouble, when Momma's mind had been possessed elsewhere.

. . .

It was some shock, I tell you, when there we were, Mark and Tim and I, sitting stuffing ourselves with popcorn enjoying *Flames in the Icehouse* at the old Bijou Palace in Evansville, and on comes this real gorgeous creature and I let out a scream: "Easter! It's your Auntie Easter!" And it was—our Easter, acting up a storm, alive and well and in the movies. A small storm for sure, but storm it was, with a credit at the end and all: Noel Sargent, her stage name, as they say, fancy as all get-out, but our Easter beyond a doubt.

Momma went wild when we ran home and told her. She didn't get a wink of sleep all night and was down there in the a.m. long before the theater opened, spooking around and making a spectacle of herself hammering and scratching at the box office window even though not a soul had showed up yet. She sat through that movie four times, right straight through until the movie palace closed, and got home so plumb exhausted she passed out on the morris chair before making it to her bed. Slept there all night until next a.m. and went right down without making breakfast, and that's what she did every precious day until the movie changed and the next show came in.

Momma lived surrounded by love right up to the end. All of us did her proud, all except Easter, who never came back though we were sure she would. Even when Momma lay dying on her bed of pain and I kept trying to reach Easter, the closest I could get to her was her lawyer, Mr. Gregson Bautzer, who told me to stop pestering Miss Sargent—some nerve—because she had no mother or kin and if it was money we were after, there were ways of putting a stop to that: his exact words! It's not money, you shit, I told him, but he hung up on me like I was some pesky fan and right after that Momma got worse and a few hours later passed on to wherever it is we all pass on to —heaven in Momma's case—still looking toward the door, trusting right up to the end that it would open and there would be Easter running through that door, saying, "Momma—I've come home."

Jess

That time I met Mac in Los Angeles. There had been a mix-up about hotels and we ended up at the Beverly Wilshire, in the new wing. It wasn't the first time we'd been on a trip together but it was the first time he hadn't been on assignment. He'd taken time off, and there we were Thursday through Monday. In and out, driving here and there, turning on the radio and each time it was blaring forth "Hopelessly Devoted to You," and in the night turning in sleep one toward the other after the wild sweetness of him inside me. It had been a hasty kind of move, this trip, and I'd thrown things into a duffel at the last minute and taken off. In my haste I'd panicked and thrown in too many shoes, and there they were on the closet floor of Room 470, all eight pairs neatly in a row.

"What's Billie's real name?" I said.

We were having dinner at the Bistro and I felt easy saying it, asking him, even though it always depressed him to bring her up.

"Willa. Willa Mae."

"Willa," I said. "Oh."

I kept on. "Of course—a Willa would naturally become a Bill, I mean a Billie."

"Let's order dinner," he said, and that's what we did.

Willa—I hadn't expected that at all. Quite a cut-up as a child no doubt, with frisky little ways meriting something cuter than the solemn Willa. Yes, nicknames tend to stick. She became Billie and Willa only surfaces on serious documents—checks and joint tax returns, things like that.

Willa Mae Hollis.

But why torment myself.

We had a fight on that trip. Over some silly thing, I can't even remember now what it was. Only how it ended—in bed, of course.

Sunday around eleven we drove to Venice Beach. (Driving he always takes my hand and tools along with the other hand on the wheel.) The sun at the beach was blinding, and the sweater I wore was too hot, but I kept it on anyway—block letters were woven into the beige wool in soft red: PARADISE.

He parked the car and we breezed down the strip of pavement by the beach, his arm around me. The houses were strung along the shore like facades from silent-film studio lots, but here people lived. Through a doorway a glimpse of someone reading tarot, a gypsy with a child leaning sleepily against her, weight lifters, mimes with their irritating demands for attention, booths selling jewelry made of bones. A massive door cemented in the sand, perversely placed catty-corner against the ocean, gave pause—NO EXIT blazed above it in neon, flashing on and off. Suddenly, ahead, crowds parted to make way for a wheelchair pushed smoothly along by a black giant on roller skates, bald, serene. His charge: a Pre-Raphaelite princess, her destroyed face radiant in its madness, eyes gazing into eternity, the tangled seaweed of her hair floating against the blue sky. She sat thin and straight, palms upward on the arms of the chair (as if to receive the stigmata). As they glided by, her eyes seared through to that which was lost long ago—and I saw as in a fun-house mirror my mother, Dolores. I turned to Mac. "Do you suppose they're from central casting?"

It came out easily. I laughed.

"Look, Jessa!" He nodded toward a freak twisting in the sand, doing a jig to a merry accordion, but I pulled him away, not wanting to look, not wanting to be drawn into the quicksand of another's pain, not that day . . .

We walked back to the car and drove to the hotel for room-service lunch. After, we made love and after that went to see *Grease* in a shopping mall. The only seats left were in the front row but we took them anyway and sprawled out holding hands, craning our necks at the screen. Sitting beside us were two fat girl twins stuffing their faces with jelly doughnuts, their heads lolling back on the seats. We laughed a lot and drove back to the hotel and made love again before going to a Mexican place for dinner, quite late.

I woke in the night . . . I reached for Mac in the darkness but there was no one, and when I turned on the light the room was empty. He was gone.

Is that my mother disappearing through the alley of cypress trees in the hot garden? It is August but she glides, a cool white bird, through the green, past the hollyhocks white and cool on their tall green stems. I run after her, too late! Petals fall from the white-flowering trees, or is it snow I run through, calling out: Wait!

The Diaries of Dolores Willis

THE GORKY SANITARIUM

I told them I wanted to make doodles to keep my mind going and I waited and waited and after days went by they gave me a copybook with every page a blank and here I sit turning one after the other with my thoughts white and blank as the pages I turn. Well—I could write my name at the top—Dolores Figueroa Willis. And then what? When I got here they behaved as if there was something wrong with me, as if I belonged here with the others. Some are quite odd, but to be fair, not all are, most are only so-sos like me. I've heard that crazy people never really know they are, so who's to say? My closest friend here is called Brillianta Vosvi and she doesn't think I'm odd at all but then she's crazy, so as I said, who knows? They treat us well, speaking as we do in many tongues, some might call it babbling but to us it's communication. Yes, close bonds of communication are forged in this place of places, no one ever says Good-bye, because no one ever seems to leave or go away unless they die maybe.

I keep writing to Nico. Oh, they take my letters, all right, but they must drop them into a well because he never answers. I haven't heard from him, much less anyone else. He loves me, he really does, I know he does, but if so why am I here? Why isn't he down there at the bottom of the well with his hands reaching up waiting to catch my letters? Something must have happened. Just when it starts coming to me milk pours over images and my mind is white again, blank as the next page.

They have us working in the garden on pretty days. Brillianta has pretty eyes, olive eyes. They remind me of someone, only hers are darker. Jessica maybe. But I can't remember who she was. Right now, that is. Other days I can.

How bright the light is on the white pebbles around the flower beds. I'd steal one but there are no pockets on these sacks we wear. They're scratchy as sandpaper and have stripes on them so we all look like zebras shuffling around only ours are black, green and white with nowhere to put anything in much less hide it. So I content myself by patting the pebbles warmed by the sun, so soft and smooth I pretend it's skin I pat and that my hand is Nicolai's hand touching my face. But I pat pat pat too hard and it's not skin at all, only old stones I slap, cold stones jumbled together that hurt my hand until someone says stop that! Once—maybe twice—Brillianta Vosvi threw some at me. Look, I screamed, it's not confetti. That night I had a dream, all my hair fell out, handfuls of it. What a mess. God knows where Brillianta went. I really got mad at her that time but now she's back and it's all forgotten, smoothed over just like the pebbles and she's her own crazy self again.

Brillianta calls me Madre. Isn't that a hoot?

Jess

"Are you getting fed up with me?" Mac said.

He's said this from time to time, and I've always answered: "No, I'm not."

"Good," he'll say, putting the matter to rest.

And that's that until the next time.

But *was* it good? Sometimes it was and sometimes it wasn't, and when it wasn't I'd decide it was time to go, that nothing between us was leading anywhere.

It was during one of those times that Felice introduced me to someone, and so there was a lot that pushed me toward him (friends mainly), but there were other things about him that gave considerable pause. As Molly put it: "So you want to live in California?" He did live in Los Angeles. There was that to contend with, along with a house best described as Beverly Hills throughout. There were overstuffed seating groups facing shelves holding morocco-bound books (unread) and a screen that eased electronically down for the showing of the after-dinner "motion picture." There was an exercise room with its gadgetry and its hermetically sealed environment, and art of the moment purchased for investment purposes (only), and a game room for poker nights (Mondays and Wednesdays, and Saturday afternoons), and butlers, cooks and maids to make things run smoothly, coming and going like extras from last week's shooting. He was rumored to be "quite rich," but over his money hung something unpleasant, misuse of funds, em-bezzlement perhaps? Something like that, but the little principality of the town for one reason or another had rallied round, saying he'd been driven to such extremes by loyalty, bravely taking the rap for a friend, whatever—so there he was, a widower presented as a Beverly Hills prince and "quite a catch." Off-putting as all this was, I started serious conversations with myself (egged on by Felice), editing out the things about him I wasn't attracted to, hoping that after this was done there would be values left to trust.

Soon after we met he flew across the country to take me out to dinner (and incidentally so Katie could give him the once-over). He was on the dot of eight and when I walked into the living room he was looking down at his Guccis inching over the Aubusson, meticulously seeking out creaks in the floor beneath.

"Your parquet creaks," he said.

He kept noodling around over the garlanded Aubusson, discovering more creaks, and I found myself explaining that the building was an old one, about to add, "No creaks in Beverly Hills parquet, I imagine," but I held my tongue so as not to start the evening off on a snippy note.

He was outfitted dapper as could be, initials on shirt cuffs— what did the middle Z stand for? The overfitted suit accentuated the porcine shape of his body, and as I looked at the ovoid face, noticing once again that his eyes were too close together— definitely too close—I had an insane impulse to pull at his face as if it were putty, put it right. But the hand with pinkie-ringed finger: what to do about that?

The moment we got in the car he reached for the phone.

"I'm calling my office, Jess," he said, oozing himself with a plumply pleased manner into the soft burgundy Ultrasuede of the seat. "You don't mind, do you, darling?"

It seems he was much preoccupied with the seating arrangements for a dinner he was giving at Spago for one hundred fifty guests two days hence and he prattled on, saying things like "No, no, dear"—he put one hand over the receiver and winked at me: "Debbie's new on the job"—"no, no, Debbie, put him on hold, stick him on the 'B' waiting list until you hear if Robert Wagner can't come, then O.K. go go go green light invite invite."

He was quite caught up in this problem of too many single women and a shortage of men to balance the seating . . . On and on it went in that vein, while I kept crossing and uncrossing my legs, annoyed with myself for being so fidgety.

At Le Cirque, Serio greeted him warmly and showed us to a corner table. This pleased him inordinately and he gazed around the room, satisfied that the evening was progressing as planned. I wasn't going to give his eyes another thought, but the square diamond on the pinkie kept flashing as he twiddled at a poppy-seed roll. After all, eyes close together were such a cliché they should be dismissed, so I must concentrate on the task at hand, which was to fall in love. Yes, there was no doubt about it—this man sitting next to me could turn into an object of serious affection. Even piggy eyes could become lovable in time on the right person, and I drifted back to looking at a girl sitting directly opposite us . . .

I'd noticed her the moment we came in, for she had an uncanny resemblance to a girl Mac and I had seen once in an overcrowded airport as we'd sat waiting to board a plane.

"Did you notice that girl?" he'd said.

I hadn't, but yes—the face without guile, an openness . . .

"Icelandic?" he'd mused. "Swedish perhaps?"

Teasingly I'd almost said, "Do you fancy her?"

Yes, there was no mistaking it. It was she.

"That's why I gamble," he was saying. We'd come to the end of dinner, dawdling over coffee.

"Yes, precisely." He was smoothing his thumb over the diamond on the pinkie ring in a meditative mood. "It's not having what I want in my life that makes me gamble."

He looked at me with a piggy gaze of great significance.

I fiddled with the sliver of lemon in my demitasse. "Is that what keeps gamblers gambling?" I asked.

He didn't answer.

"Because I've never been able to understand gambling. It's somehow getting something for nothing. That's if you win, of course, but maybe it's about losing—not winning: the risk of starting from the beginning, the thrill of another chance."

He didn't take to that notion at all. "I never think about things like that," he said, dismissing it with a wave of his cigar. "I'd stop in a minute if I had what I wanted."

"And what's that?"

"You," he said quickly. Too quickly.

But I was barely listening, for I'd started tormenting myself about the girl sitting across from us: her heart-shaped face with high cheekbones, the skin luminous in the candlelight as suddenly she turned and looked directly at us as if she had recognized me. Had her gray eyes been suffused with joy as Mac held her against the cold cold icy white of winter in Iceland where volcanic white-blue light spreads across the land? Had he watched her face when she came to him as so often he had watched mine?

Later, he said, "Together you and I will know everything in the world there is to know."

Impressive, isn't it?

He was trying to make love to me.

The Diaries of Dolores Willis

THE GORKY SANITARIUM

This place I'm visiting must have been a palace once and the room I'm in probably a maid's room. There's something about the other rooms that reminds me of a place I've lived in before, but which place or where? On some days I'm sixteen and back at the convent again, other days not, because the Mother Superior here is a Father Superior, but there are other Superiors that go to and fro as the nuns did, their rosaries click clicking castanets, always on the move, doing one thing or another. My room is hardly what I'm used to but is acceptable in its way. The narrow bed with its thin mattress is surprising. Though it looks hard, what with the metal headboard, it's not too bad to flounce around on—or fold my hands across my chest and pretend I'm dead. Sarah Bernhardt used to do that, only she lay down in a coffin so it's not the same. When I open my eyes and look up at the crucifix hanging on the wall over my bed there's only a white space.

The thing I miss most is not being able to go to Antoine's. No one comes to wash our hair or do our nails and as for a pedicure, forget it. No maintenance around here, that's the problem. I should report this, only I don't know which Superior to report it to. The Father wouldn't have a clue—anyway he's got other things on his mind. Brillianta Vosvi is no help at all. She couldn't care less what her hair looks like, much less what a pedicure is. Did I tell you about her teeth? I must have. Anyway, she'd be quite pretty if she fixed herself up, but then comes the smile and what to do, not to mention the hair in two long stringy braids. Well, that could be washed every day and left to fluff dry, still it wouldn't get anywhere near where the trouble is, because even with all that fluffiness around her face she'd smile, and there they'd be, one dried raisin after another. Of course here no one thinks a thing of it, because almost every-body has a false tooth or two dotted among the real ones and they're made of iron. Isn't that something? Of course after a while you get used to it—everywhere you look half-moon smiles filled with rice pudding, a dried raisin here and there popping out at you.

No raisins, I tell Brillianta: when people smile in America, not a one. Teeth, even if false, are white as can be in America, white as you could wish, creamy white as mine, which are real of course, but even if they weren't no one could tell the dif-ference. That's the way we do things in America, I tell her. To make her absolutely ecstatic all I have to do is open my mouth wide and let her tap tap my teeth. "A-me-ri-ca?" she says, covetously counting them, pestering to hear more. But her tapping soon wearies me and I shut my mouth and say, later, later, leave Dolores alone.

How suspicious Nico was! But I knew I could win him, turn him around, it was only a matter of time. In the beginning it was a game, a game I knew I could win. And then I did, so it wasn't a game anymore.

· · ·

Oh God, dawn filtering through the jalousies of my sleeping chamber, April light, the bowl of *muguet* as he kissed me, the sweetness of knowing it was not the last, for he would return that night to quench my thirst. And there would always be more, but it was never enough, never enough to quench the fever that consumed us both. Deep breaths I'd take, satiated yet wanting more. What did I care about their warnings, Nadezhda Plevitskaya and the others: all of them kept telling me to stay away from him, that he was a Communist, close to Stalin and God knows what else, but I didn't listen, cared nothing about any of it, all I cared about was him. Eyes like steel, yes, but not to me. He found the gentleness in me, the gentleness, so much there, the beauty for him, all of it, only for him, and he softened, slowly slowly. I could see it happening although no one else did, no one else knew. Outwardly he was unchanged. How thrilling this secret Nico, this man known only to me, the real Nicolai Voznesensky. And for him . . . the secret places in me, the tenderest love I had never given to anyone, never suspected was in me—no, not in *that* way: now for him alone. Yes, all.

There were no boundaries in this kingdom of bliss, for I was no longer myself, in some unfathomable way I had merged into him, become him—so simple, as natural as breathing, there was no need to make mention or say anything of it, each to the other. I knew he knew, for he started trusting me. His words drifted through my head as the gentle flutter of a fan of silk, back and forth, to and fro, held by an unseen hand—mine?— fading and disappearing into a summer night. It was my presence in that quiet listening world which was of utmost importance to him, necessary to him. Mine alone the power to soothe and replenish, so he returned to Moscow refreshed for the hard tasks demanded of him. Yes, in some mysterious way, the one who spoke and the one who listened were the same.

There's a reason why I'm here and if I can remember I'll be able to tell Father Superior and he'll let me out. He and the other Superiors pretend they don't know who Nicolai Voznesensky is, but it's a lie. Everybody knows who he is, though important why or to whom? Something to do with Stalin— Thank God I wrote it down somewhere.

There's a change in Brillianta Vosvi lately. She washes her hair whenever they let her and takes pride in brushing it dry in the sunlight. Much time is spent looking at herself in whatever she can get her hands on to reflect an image, studying how her face changes when she smiles. She dotes on hearing about creams and unguents, beauty secrets, and is certain I'm writing them down in this book, which she's dying to get her hands on. But it's easy to divert her by describing other mysteries, leg waxings and so forth. I don't want her or anyone else to read this.

I was wrong about one thing—some do leave this place and they don't have to die to do it, because they come around to say *"Do svidaniya."* After that there's a gap, someone you saw yesterday isn't here today, someone you see tomorrow may be gone next month, next year. But who decides, Brillianta Vosvi? Who decides who gets out and why? She grabbed my hand and quickly pulled me toward her, hissing in my ear, "You have to get to be one of *them* instead of one of *us*."

She's much crazier than I gave her credit for.

Brillianta Vosvi

It annoyed me when Dolores first heard my name and asked me if it was my real name for although it is true my father wanted to call me Anna and fanciful names are not encouraged in our country Brillianta is the name given to me at birth. A gypsy predicted to my mother that I would be a girl and luck and good fortune would follow if I was named Brillianta. How mistaken she was! But no matter, I still haven't lost hope. Another story my mother used to tell me was about the Witch Baby. This particular baby eats its parents with iron teeth. If my mother were alive this never would be. Even if I had gobbled her up she would never have let them put me here in the Gorky.

Dolores puts all her beauty secrets down in her notebooks. Someday she's going to let me read them. There are places in America and elsewhere called beauty salons where women can go and be made beautiful. When I get out of here I'm going to one and see what happens, but first I'll get my teeth fixed so they look like hers. Dolores says they have rinses at these salons of beauty to make the hair soft as goo-foo feathers.

What are goo-foo feathers?

"Oh, you know," she said, and that was the end of that.

There are places where I fade away and when I sense this is happening I know once again the quicksand has got hold of me and is sucking me down for I am choking and cannot swallow the sand. Then I wake up, but I don't know where I've been or how long I've been gone, only that I'm back and that it is because of my brother Miron Semenovich that I am here, in this place.

These are things I do not believe in: Petit-Bourgeois Laxity,

Spinelessness, Vacillation, Disorganization, Anarchy, Individualism, and so on. This is what Lenin taught us. But now he is dead and so are Stalin and the rest. We have a new *Vozhd*— Gorbachev, our chief leader, who also has utopian goals for us. Who knows how far the innovations have progressed?

Yes, it is because of my brother Miron Semenovich Vosvi that I am here. He is a senior associate at the Medical and Biological Institute of Moscow University. He knows what's what, I can tell you, is always on the right side, always lands on his feet. How do I know these things? Because I am his sister, and just because I'm a guest here at the Gorky doesn't mean I'm not.

Actually, my mother is not dead and she knows my whereabouts. I also lied about Miron Semenovich. He is only indirectly responsible for my being here. There are other reasons, which I will reveal in due course. Matters pertaining to the bird that was inserted into my head and left there. A small bird, a canary perhaps, although obviously, as I could not see it, I was not positive of correct identification. By its song, however, I could surmise that it was not a pigeon with seductive cooings nor the supreme nightingale, whose melody I am well acquainted with. No, it produced the superficial warbling of a canary, trilled without cease, day and night, up and down, trapped in my poor little head round and round, trying to get out. Other times it would rest, but even then the singing went on, uninterrupted as before. Finally it was too much for me and I told my mother about this awful situation, only to have her make light of it, believing me to be up to my old tricks and whimsical ways, but after a time she saw how pale I was getting without sleep, unable to eat and so on. At this time I was teaching at a special school where all instruction is carried on in one foreign language or another. Luckily the classes I was in charge of were in English, otherwise Dolores and I wouldn't have been able to communicate in the close way that we do, although her French and German are fluent, and she understands more Russian than she lets on. Anyway, teaching classes of forty-two children six hours a day six days a week with the canary singing in my head is what finally did me in. This yellow bird was put in position by my husband, whom I had recently divorced. Unlike some of my other friends, I had been married only twice. As divorce was available by a request from either party without notice having to be given, the procedure took only a few minutes. He was in a fit because I divorced him without so much as a hint of my intent and the outcome of this fury was that he revenged himself against me. Coward that he is, he plotted to do this while I slept, for the canary was there singing away, woke me up in fact, the day after I divorced him. At the time I was living with my parents, having gone there after the trouble. How he sneaked in and out without anyone knowing is one of the mysteries. Anyway, it was my father who told my brother Miron Semenovich of what had been perpetrated and he quickly introduced me to a highly respected colleague at the Medical Institute so I had someone other than my mother with whom to go into the ins and outs of what had taken place. It was this colleague that I begged for the operation that would cut into my head. I didn't care how they got in, just get in and let the damn thing out, I told him. I also insisted that, no matter how repellent it was, he should put the creature immediately into a cage placed by my bed so I could view my tormentor the moment I returned from anesthesia. This was imperative because I wanted it to be my own hand that let the thing out of the cage to fly away, each of us to be free of the other at last.

It was soon after this canary episode that Dolores and I became comrades. No one was witness to this, for we inched toward each other gradually until one day, there we were close confidantes, as if it had always been thus. By the time I got here she had been a resident of the Gorky since who knows when and fitted into the daily ups and downs as if she belonged, quite a favorite with one and all. Not that favoritism was encouraged—we all had intense preoccupations of our own what with one thing and another. That she had once been most beautiful was apparent to all, and even now she might glance away or at you in a certain way and for a moment beauty comes upon her again but fleetingly the way a grasshopper in the garden hops in and out of view, or the shape of a cloud changes from ogre to unicorn before it drifts into nothingness.

She prefers to communicate in English, and although there are others among us who speak many languages, it is to me she is most attracted. And I to her. Until I arrived she was withdrawn, selective in her ways, perhaps even snooty? Yes, we have singled each other out and I am delighted by her manner and the way she has of putting things. There is something about her unlike anyone I've ever met and so as the years pass I find ways to attach myself to her more and more—yes, more than anything I intend to be her friend.

Why do I merit her favor? Whenever I'm about to ask her we seem to get off on other tangents. She writes many letters, waits for answers that never arrive. As for those books she writes in, someday she'll trust me enough to let me get my hands on them. Sometimes she talks about this man she's in love with, Nico, saying he'll be here soon to take her away, very powerful, this Nico, so powerful he'll get us both out. But when I demand details she only smiles and says:

"*Morozhenoe.*"

Ice cream? What has that to do with it?

. . .

Something set her off this morning and she pressed her hands over her ears, bobbing her head from side to side, tick tock tick tock—something about children, children and earthworms they were given, earthworms to eat! She sobbed and sobbed and I knew she'd break in two or three or four pieces. So I tried to comfort her but someone came and interrupted us, taking her away, and I haven't seen her for two days. Or is it years?

Jess

NEW YORK CITY

It's the middle of December. I've asked Ken's advice about what to say next time Mac calls. Ken makes suggestions, which I write down.

"Look, Mac" (Ken's good at this), "the holidays are difficult. Abe died on Christmas Day. I have a lot of work to do, a lot going on in my life (including you), and I'm putting everything on hold until after the new year. I have things to sort out and so do you. Katie's debut with Baryshnikov is not far off and I've got the American Impressionist show at the gallery and I don't want to deal with anything else."

This helps organize my thoughts, but knowing that just hearing his voice I'll forget most of it, I write it down. When he calls he keeps interrupting:

"But do you love me? do you love me?"

And I do. Love him. So I write a letter, a letter he'll never read because it's over.

Mac— It's dawn and the light across the river is of a palest apricot, fading into aqua, and soon it will be day. You were right about Monday a week ago when you couldn't reach me by phone until late—too late for us to meet. I had decided not to see you again. But now, as that "grey dawn" of Masefield you love so well "is breaking," I'm thinking of the shock of recognition when my eyes first looked upon your face and I don't despair. I have faith in the inevitability of you and me. As for your Protestant guilt—well that will be there always, more or less, probably more, but don't shut me out because of it, please don't. I understand everything, I truly do.

Instead of counting sheep I lie in the dark counting relics I may or may not throw away:

Collection of doodles drawn on the pad by my bed as he checks his answering service—variations of Boon with a scribbled "my friend" underneath, but sometimes not. Another: Boon, a ball at random, a scythe with crossed dagger, a curtain parted, and in the corner, "Artist unknown," with a circle dot over the *i*.

His toothbrush.

A message, folded fortune-cookie size and held by a red paper clip, which I'd intended to give him with a promise not to read it until he got to Managua.

Mac
Did you ever believe
in love that lasts forever?
Do you still?

Something must have happened or else why do I have this last scrap? Now I remember. He was going to stop by on his way to the airport very early in the morning. But he didn't.

On the terrace in moonlight, the pillow soft he placed beneath me, soft still as I press my face into it in darkness. Nothing has changed.

Jane

LONDON

So just as we're doing the usual settling in again we're setting out—Jane Esmond's off to America for location shooting in New York. Grafton's used to it, this restless coming and going, but Garnet is more home-minded than we two. Not home-minded enough to want Grafton and me to stay with her in New York, however.

"It just wouldn't work, Grafton!" she said, not taking to the idea at all.

Grafton sat there mildly amused by this little domestic scene, certain it was about to turn into a tug-of-war between Garnet and me as to whom he'd stay with in New York.

"Buzz off," I told them. "I'll get my own place—with my schedule I'll need space and time for myself, so who cares."

"Absolutely!" Garnet said quickly, but Grafton just turned away.

Later, on our way out to dinner, he informed us he'd probably be staying on at the flat in London, for a time at least. But perhaps not.

"It depends on a lot of things," he said.

"What things?"

He shrugged while Garnet turned her nose—exquisite—up in the air and looked into space as if she hadn't heard any of it.

Next day when I got back from the studio I could feel the emptiness the minute I walked in, a big empty pocket. Grafton was in the kitchen nursing his hangover, making tea, and there wasn't a trace of Garnet anywhere.

"She left you something." He took an envelope out from under a biscuit tin.

Jane had been scrawled rather hastily across it, and I went into the bathroom and closed the door so he wouldn't be spooking around while I read it.

Jane—

I don't really know why I keep coming here—it is a mistake. It's best we don't see each other again. I don't much care if I see Grafton again either. I know I've said that before and it always seems to turn out otherwise. But this time I mean it. There are times I wish we'd met under different circumstances—you and me. I've come to like you, respect you certainly more than I do Grafton, but then I'm in love with him (sometimes) and that complicates everything. Anyway, there's no reason to prolong this, I only meant to say Good-bye.

Garnet

Grafton's been impossible since she left. Well, go! Go after her! I want to scream at him, but instead Jelly-Jane dons her knickers and playacts a bit and some of the impossibleness gets sidetracked for a while. Tomorrow's the day we leave—the cast, that is—for New York and the Wyndham Hotel, where we'll be based. Grafton's been mumbling about his New York gallery and some group show, so who knows what he'll do. I almost hope he stays on in London, at least for a while. I've about exhausted my repertoire.

Garnet

NEW YORK CITY

I felt free on the plane, so free getting on, getting off, running free at the airport as the customs man stamped my passport saying:

"Welcome home!"

For days after I never gave Grafton and Jane a thought— only a blink back sometimes, wondering what they were up to. Colors I painted—magenta, the orange next to it taking my breath away—rejoicing in being alone, in being Garnet again, after the fever, yes white hot fever, of that white, white world where I'd been unable to move or think or do anything but thirst for more.

Still, as time goes by, alone with my work, I find the two of them coming back into my thoughts. Not when I'm painting but in moments between when I'm doing nothing. I'll be lying on the sofa and there they'll be. First Grafton and then sooner or later Janey popping in with her yellow hair. I've started painting her.

Not a word from either of them. I wonder if she showed him my letter. I can't even remember now what I said. Something about Good-bye. Oh well.

Letters to a stranger. A woman named Garnet. Someone I keep meeting now and again, unexpectedly—so she's not a stranger. Who is she? Why does she keep them?

Philadelphia
Wednesday

Benefit audience at the matinee today. All those women in their hats and gloves with the herd trooping back, oooing and ahhing, to get a close-up look at me after the performance. Ah, my dear—if only you were as taken with me as these silly things.

Q

Friday

You do understand, don't you—about Molly. If ever I was going to get married it was time, and although the passion was minimal she's a good sort, I thought, and we like each other and maybe that's all there is, so why not. Then three months later you walked into the room at that boring party and we started talking and I knew that wasn't all.

Q

Saturday

I think about you all the time. Last night at curtain call I thought I saw you in the second row. I was sure it was you. Then she turned in profile and of course it wasn't, didn't look anything like you at all. God, how I miss you.

Q

Monday

Darling, are you well?

Q

Thursday

Garnet, you hold back because I'm married, because you don't really know me yet. These are things you say but do you mean them really? All I want is to let myself love you—that will be the real Quentin Jones, not the impostor that the fools see on the stage. Oh, I'll be visible there all right but in a way that wouldn't touch my heart or the secret place that belonged to us. Think, my darling, how safe you'll be, nested in the real me. But Molly, you will say—what about that? That, dear heart, is separate, isn't it. What has it to do with the place that will be ours? Molly. She's someone I don't even like anymore.

Trust me

Q

Molly wore her Boucheron pin yesterday, which is what made me think of him again, read the letters. I'd started seeing him while she was in Europe on business. They'd recently been married but I hadn't met her, didn't know her at all, which made a difference. She was away a lot and he was about to go into rehearsal for the new Neil Simon play and he said, would I have dinner with him? After that we met often—sometimes even when she wasn't away. Actually, we were driving each other crazy, though we were just walking in the park and having hot chocolate at the zoo—that kind of thing. Then he went out of town with the play, wrote to me almost every day. I hadn't intended to see him again but when he came back he said "just lunch" and I thought why not. I had no intention of going to their apartment, but he kept insisting, wore me down, and eventually I did. Molly had been away for weeks and we were going to have lunch together and he said:

"Just stop by, pick me up here, it's on our way."

When I got there he said:

"Come in for a minute—there's something I have to show you." It was a rented apartment—surprising—a collection of ceramic poodles on the mantel all in a row. He started kissing me but I pulled away, and he went to a drawer and took out a box, black velvet, small.

"Open it," he said, smiling.

Inside was a pin, Art Deco, onyx and coral, the prettiest one I'd ever seen, exactly the sort of jewel that suits me.

"Do you like it?"

He wanted to make certain I did and said he'd searched for just the right one, it had to be perfect. On and on he went about it as I exclaimed, admired.

"Come," he said, putting his hand out, leading me across the room to where a mirror hung.

Ceremoniously he secured the pin to the lapel of my jacket,

taking time to place it delicately, just so, before turning me around to face the mirror. For an eternity we stood without saying anything. He kept smiling and I kept trying to tell him how happy I was, but other thoughts kept crowding in: I knew that soon his arms would be around me and I'd be on the floor as we had been the night before and I'd be in agony, determined again that he wasn't going to make love to me, but knowing that this time it would happen. Instead, he removed the pin gently from my jacket and went over to the desk and placed it back in its box.

"Then Molly will like it too," he said, neatly snapping the lid shut. "She'll be home tomorrow."

We walked out onto Seventy-seventh Street past the Museum of Natural History, toward Central Park West.

"I love you," he said slowly, breathing deeply, drawing it out, "but I'm not going to leave her."

"Oh, I know that," I said.

None of it mattered now anyway, because I'd given nothing of myself to him, no, nothing, nothing at all.

Of course all that was long ago, before Molly and I became friends. But he was the first. The first of the kind of man who attracts me, gets to me in a way others don't.

"That was quite an acceptance speech when he got the Oscar last year," Molly said.

"Do you ever run into him?" I asked her.

"No, praise be! It surprises me he's never married again."

"Wed to Quentin Jones, I daresay."

"Thank God we didn't have any children," Molly said, turning away. "That's a life sentence, and he really was awful!"

Claude Lubin called a minute ago; we're going to an opening at the Weatherbee Galleries before dinner. We almost got together years ago, but he was too caught up elsewhere: all he wanted to do was talk about her. Maybe we did go to bed once. It's hard for me to remember what anyone is like except Grafton. And Jane. He told me I'd be meeting the woman he was so in love with. Finally I'm going to meet her—Jessica Weatherbee.

Jess

Claude showed up at the gallery for the opening. It was already crowded, but I spotted him the minute he arrived—with a woman who drew me to her by an invisible string, a willing fish for the catch. I knew why, of course. She reminded me of someone, a photograph actually—a photograph I have of my mother. Then, when she spoke, her voice had the same soft sound I remembered, even the slight stammer now and again, shy almost. How could anyone so exquisite be shy, but of course that has nothing to do with anything. Claude couldn't not be aware of it. The resemblance. Odd he never mentioned it. It's something he'd know would interest me, interest me enormously. I still feel guilty about last fall when I broke off with Mac (or tried to) and spent the night with Claude. It wasn't fair to be doing that, using him, and after Mac and I came together again (as we always do), I sometimes brooded over what had happened between Claude and me, thinking maybe I should go back to him so that I could somehow put it right, although I know of course things don't work that way.

Her name is Garnet, Garnet Blackburn.

Garnet

"Garnet, what did you think of Jess?" Claude asked.

She has the most extraordinary eyes—olive—set in her face at a slightly askew tilted-down angle that should be all wrong, but it's not. It's exactly right.

Instead, I said, "Are you still in love with her?"

But he wasn't listening, eager to tell me something: "She told me you remind her of someone . . . her mother."

"Her *mother*?"

"Yes—Dolores Willis. She was a great beauty, so you can be pleased."

"Really?"

"Jess has photographs of her all around her house. It helps her to accept things."

"Accept things? What things?"

"Oh—it's ancient history now, but in the thirties it was an international cause célèbre. Jess's father was a political big wheel named Drew Willis, who was killed when his yacht sank, and right after that her mother took Jess to Europe. They moved around with the seasons—London, Monte Carlo, Deauville in summer, that sort of thing. Then one day, when Jess was about six, Dolores disappeared without a trace. There were all sorts of wild rumors, that she was a spy for the Russians and who knows what else. Nothing was ever proven, but to this day no one knows what really happened."

How intriguing, I thought, my resemblance to the mysterious missing Dolores, though I couldn't help wondering if I'd agree—it's awfully risky telling someone he looks like someone else. Quite often it's a shock and then it turns out the other person's not at all a mirror image of the way he perceives himself. Certainly I wouldn't mind resembling *Jess*, though, with those olive eyes set in a face that has the simple directness of a folk painting. There's something very real about her—*too* real. A trait to be admired, but it can get you in a lot of trouble . . . And that lemony hair—that looks real too.

"Now I'm getting curious," I said to Claude.

"Easily taken care of—I'm sure Jess'd love to show you the pictures of her mother."

"Well," I said, not wanting to get too involved, "perhaps. Let's see what happens."

Jess

My mother, Dolores Willis, had lots of admirers everywhere and the rooms were full of people coming and going—a party all the time. I'd see her from a distance drifting in and out of rooms or up a staircase, down a hall, disappearing behind the door of her bedroom. There'd be laughter and then silence. Once I tried to follow but the door was locked.

I made her nervous I think. No wonder. She must have caught on early that I wanted something from her that she couldn't give. I should have let her be, but I couldn't do that, it wasn't in my nature.

I don't remember my father at all. If he'd been around it would have been different. Maybe. I used to pretend this or that one was my father, but they came and went one after the other and the moving around didn't help. Anyway, it was my mother who preoccupied me all the time in one way or another.

I wanted to *be* her—not just be *like* her. When she went

away it happened quickly so it took a long time to sink in—gone! Even when it did, I still didn't believe it. But maybe that's because I was a child. Time and the space it took up in a day meant nothing. The loss of her was there the way a clock is there, sitting on a mantel or hanging on a wall ticking away, what matter? The hands point to twelve as it chimes, but is it night or morning? One interchangeable with the other. It didn't mean she wasn't coming back.

After she went away they questioned me about her—baby questions that made me angry. You tell *me*, you tell *me*, I wanted to scream at them. This went on for days and days. But finally it stopped. There wasn't anything I could tell them anyway. I knew a lot about her but it was hidden, secret knowledge, in a language I couldn't translate. She hadn't left a note or anything. One day she just wasn't there. But I kept pretending that any day she'd be back, the way I did after Abe died—precisely.

After the questions stopped I was sent to my father's sister to live. I was to call her Aunt Frayne and that's what I did, although I'd never met her until after it happened. She and my mother hadn't gotten along—why I don't know; anyway, that's how it was. She lived in a big house in Santa Barbara with gardens around it and a pool as big as the ocean to swim in right alongside the beach, with the ocean next to that, stretching out into the distance as far as you could see. My room faced the sea and at night it came right into my room as I lay there thinking about my mother. I'd start drowning, but I fought to stay alive because the waves were trying to tell me something, whispering, trying to get a message through from her. Then just when I'd be about to catch it, the whoosh would recede the way waves do, sucked back into the ocean to become part of something greater and disappear.

Aunt Frayne was all right in her way, I guess. What she liked to do most was play cards with her friends. She was also interested in having her hair done, and every morning Miss Rita came to the house to do this. Aunt Frayne would send the car and chauffeur to pick her up at ten without fail, Sundays too, to get Aunt Frayne ready for her busy day with her friends. Her hair always looked the same, pasted down, more like a wig than hair. She wore reddish-brown lipstick of a similar shade and it traveled up over the top of her lip as wiggly pathways do on a map, only these led nowhere. She did try. To be nice to me. But when she talked to me it was to a child. How could she know that I was already a grownup—a grownup in a child's body, counting the days until I could get out? Nothing she could have said would have made a difference anyway, because all I wanted to talk about was my mother and what had happened. At the same time, if Aunt Frayne or anyone else had attempted this I would have slammed the door, because not to talk about it made it better. Maybe none of it was true. Still I kept waiting, but all I got was a sigh now and again to her friends about my father:

"Ah, dear Drew! such a great statesman, such a loss to our great nation."

Then she'd drift on to something else. Not that I could have talked about him anyway. What was there to say about any of it?

The Diaries of Dolores Willis

THE GORKY SANITARIUM

The more I put on a page the more things come back to me. Then I get tired and put the book down and everything disappears like it's been erased and I stare at it wondering—what? So I open it again to a page and read aloud to myself, saying, So there! Dolores Willis does exist after all.

What year is it, Brillianta Vosvi?

"Year?" She shrugged. Then she started talking in one of the strange tongues in which she's fluent. No, I said sternly, I mean it! What year is it? So she held up her hand slowly, counting her fingers: one two three . . . and just as she got to ten one of those damn bells rang—time for tea and yogurt.

In the courtyard as we walk it keeps going around and around in my head: "And I keep in the squares, / And the masses of bears, / Who wait at the corners all ready to eat / The sillies who tread on the lines of the street . . ." Lots of bears around this place, I can tell you.

I'm going to write a letter to Drew. Maybe it's only the dead who receive letters.

Drew darling,
 How are you? It's been quite a while since we talked to each other. You were always busy and then when we did get together there wasn't much to say. Those long pauses at twenty minutes past the hour when they say "an angel must be passing over." Lots of angels in our day—right? Lots around here too. It's either feast or famine, with lots of chitchat or lots of empty silence, just sitting around. What was it like when the boat sank? Please write and tell me. It's a subject that piques my curiosity. Was there

a lot of screaming or did everyone put their arms around whoever happened to be next to him and say I love you? Drew, I want to go home. Please come and take me there. If you can't yourself have someone else do it. I'll tell you more about everything when I see you.

Hugs, kisses and God bless,
Dolores

Jess

NEW YORK CITY

When I was nine, I guess it was around then, I started having a recurrent dream and there I'd be, back once again in the house in Paris with my mother before it happened, before she disappeared. As it was in the present, nothing had happened yet, but it was going to, and in the dream I knew this. Something was going to happen, and I could *prevent* it from happening, only I couldn't, because it was in the future and I had no way of knowing what it was. And when I'd wake up, it was the house by the sea in Santa Barbara and Aunt Frayne that were the dream, not real life at all—*real* life was the dream I'd come from. About this time I started knowing my mother wasn't coming back. So I had lost her. But that was O.K., wasn't it, because if you lose something you can find it again, and even though no one knew what had happened to her, even if some believed her dead, no one knew for certain about any of it, did they? No one except me, because I knew she existed in the dream, and if I searched long enough I'd find her and everything would be all right.

I started making lists, elaborate lists of the people she'd

known before it happened, before the disappearance. This wasn't all that easy to do. During that time I'd been two, three, four, five years old and so on, and what came to me were the faces and hats, bracelets and dresses of her friends as they came and went; names meant nothing, and as for the men, they all looked more or less alike, except Mr. Voznesensky, who I put at the very top of the very first list.

I never saw that much of Mr. Voznesensky, and what I did see I didn't care for. But to be fair that was because my mother was so in love with him. Yes, I was eaten up by jealousy. Once he came on the scene I knew I hadn't a chance to get her attention, get close to her, and that's all I cared about.

He was very important. I only found that out later, from some newspaper clippings about my mother I found in a Vuitton trunk in Aunt Frayne's basement. In one he was a "rapidly rising Communist Party official, First Vice-Chairman of SNK and an academician who writes articles for the Party journal, *Bolshevik.*" Other accounts described him as the "mastermind of Soviet industry" and "the brain behind the Soviet military-economic effort." However, that's not why he was at the top of my list. From the moment I saw them together I knew how important he was to my mother, so that's why I put him there.

Anyway, my plan was to build on these lists until I had enough information to take matters into my own hands and find her. No one knew I was doing this, of course. They'd only laugh. Who was I to succeed where the rest of the world had failed?

Since he was at the top of the list, I wrote first to Mr. Voznesensky, sending the letter care of the Russian Embassy in Paris. He'd hardly been aware of my existence, but he'd have to answer. Surely he'd remember Jessica, Dolores's daughter?

February 20, 1936

Dear Mr. Voznesensky,

I'm Dolores Willis's daughter, Jessica. I hope you don't mind my writing to you. It's about my mother. Some people think she's dead but I'm sure she's not. I keep thinking she'll be back but a lot of time has gone by and I haven't heard from her so I've decided to take things into my own hands and find her. I'm getting in touch with all the people she knew and am writing to you first because I know she loved you. I'm nine years old now but very old for my age so please answer this letter and let me know when I can see you. I live with my aunt, Mrs. Frayne, in Santa Barbara, but she's talking about a trip to Paris maybe this summer and taking me with her. I hope you remember me. I certainly remember you. Whatever you do, please answer this letter.

Yours sincerely,
Jessica Willis

Now all I had to do was wait.

The Diaries of Dolores Willis

THE GORKY SANITARIUM

She was a pretty little thing. Still it made me nervous to be around her. I was only twenty, hardly ready for a baby. Not ready at all if you really want to know. Right from the beginning it made me nervous, nervous holding her, afraid I'd drop her or something. Of course there was always one nurse or another to take over. They weren't a bit afraid of the baby—Jessica, wasn't it?—but why should they be? That's their job. Day and night, night and day, and then if one didn't suit there was always another to fill her place; they came and went. I had a staff to manage everything, and everybody around was much more able than I'd ever be to care for a baby, so it was a relief really, and I kept postponing, putting everything off—yes, that's it—postponing. Next day, next week I'd be ready, but when next day, next week came around, something always came around with it, a party or a new man or something, and what with one thing or another, it would have to be put off for later.

Paris. It was 1928. I had money, lots of it. Drew died and left it to me. I couldn't wait to get out of Washington, to get on that boat to Paris, where they said every day was the fourteenth of July. Of course I had to take the baby with me. Some of the staff too, I can't remember how many. Anyway, I found a house on the rue Jacob near Natalie Barney's but more beautiful. Lapis-lazuli columns in the ballroom, and walls of aquamarine taffeta, a background for curtains of peach-colored silk. There was a party on my birthday. Prince Hesse-Darmstadt was most attentive, a waltz, "Wien, Wien, nur du allein . . ." We were dancing, dizzy with the beauty of the music, and suddenly, standing in the doorway, in a frame of crystal light, was the dark stranger—Nicolai.

Jess

NEW YORK CITY

It was a long wait, because Mr. Voznesensky never answered.
Maybe the letter never got to him.
Maybe it did and . . . ?

. . .

No matter . . . During endless days, with these questions unanswered, I was still able to keep up with school in one way or
another as though nothing was happening (as indeed it wasn't).
On weekends, every possible moment was put into furthering
my efforts, and I can tell you it was no easy feat to keep these
activities secret from the mademoiselle governess Aunt Frayne
had engaged to keep an eye on me (an odious woman I was
instructed to address by the affectionate-sounding "Zelly").
Much time went into the scrapbook I was piecing together of
the newspaper clippings I'd found in the Vuitton trunk. Aunt
Frayne of course knew nothing of this, and I sometimes wondered if she knew anything at all about the cache of clippings—
but if not Aunt Frayne, who had collected them and so neatly
placed them in the trunk? Then there were the letters I wrote
to my mother, which I kept in a secret place until such time
as they could be presented to her by me in person; not to
mention the other letters, more or less in the genre of the one
I'd sent to Mr. Voznesensky but rephrased accordingly. The
first went to Mr. and Mrs. F. Scott Fitzgerald, who were listed
in a newspaper clipping of an account of a party given by Natalie
Barney in Paris. These parties, attended by two or three hundred
guests, were weekly occurrences every Friday between 5 p.m.
and 8, the newspaper informed me, and took place at Miss
Barney's house on the rue Jacob. On that particular Friday,
milling about inside Miss Barney's house and outside in her
garden (with its "Temple of Friendship dedicated to Sappho"),
was none other than Prince Hesse-Darmstadt in attendance
with my mother (where was Mr. Voznesensky?), who, it was
noted, wore "a Paquin gown of eau-de-Nil hue with gentle
curves reflecting the lines of architecture in the attenuated flow

of the Art Deco skyscraper" and mingled among the guests "with ease and grace," apparently without a care in the world. Once the letter to Mr. and Mrs. Fitzgerald was dispatched, there was no stopping me and I speedily wrote to others mentioned, at that gathering and others, many identified as poet, artist, et cetera. Much precious time was wasted agonizing over the hundreds who had milled around with the famous personages but not been noted in the newspaper accounts. After all, one of the unmentioned might be the very one with vital information regarding my mother. Each name I came upon pierced me with a thrill of hope, although at nine I was hard put to comprehend their significance in the grand scheme of things—historian Charles Beard, playwright Jean Jacques Bernard, Henri Bergson, Marie Laurencin, fashion designer Mainbocher, Colette and Gide, Gabriele D'Annunzio, Edna St. Vincent Millay, Jean Cocteau, Hemingway, Valéry, Edith Sitwell, Gertrude Stein, George Antheil, Ezra Pound, Carl Van Vechten and so on.

With pounding heart I sped to the library, crossing its threshold in the firm belief that what I sought waited somewhere within the pages of the hundreds of books at my disposal. Every biographical detail was of enormous significance, for there would be found if not addresses at least an indication of where to send letters to those who had seen my mother in her eau-de-Nil gown—touched her hand on that last fatal Friday. Over a period of weeks, one, two, off they went, three, four, and more letters, one after the other.

But nothing happened, nothing at all, until—just when I felt my letters were perhaps the mere scribblings of a child, the sort squashed at random into bottles and thrown desperately into the outgoing tide to toss haphazardly back and forth across cruel seas, unclaimed—an answer came.

August 15, 1936

Dear Miss Willis:

It was charming to hear from you and of course I re-member your mother Dolores Willis with admiration and affection. In fact that Friday evening at Miss Barney's mentioned in your letter your mother and I had a long conversation about the different ways of poaching pears in claret—one of my favorite desserts and hers too I was to learn. Also at the time I asked if I could photograph her which I had wanted to do ever since I had seen her as the Sun Goddess at the Beaux Arts Pageant that spring. She had a paradoxical beauty—the fire of flamenco jux-taposed against the serenity of the Madonna, but it was something else, something you can't quite catch, which fascinated. It was this illusive quality I hoped to capture in my photograph. She mentioned she was going to Vienna the next day and would be in touch when she returned a week or so later so we could arrange time mutually con-venient. However the sad circumstances intervened and I never heard from her again. I am so sorry I cannot be of more help. Your mother is much missed by all her friends. Her last words to me were "We'll meet soon, Carlo, à bientôt." You and I, Jessica, will meet one day I feel cer-tain, and, until then

Your friend,
Carl Van Vechten

This letter, under my pillow every night until it threatened to disintegrate, reluctantly found its place face down (for pri-vacy) beneath the plate glass that covered the tabletop by my bed. At night, in darkness, I would run my fingers over the glass. Mornings at sunrise, it was the first thing I touched.

Garnet

Jess Weatherbee asked me to her house for tea. I may or may not. On the one hand I'm curious to see those photographs of her mother. On the other I don't want to get involved. I've enough fantasies to preoccupy me, what with Jane and Grafton. They've drifted into my life again, at least Grafton has, with Jane always on the periphery. Not that I've seen either one since London, but Grafton keeps calling and I put him off, telling him I'm seeing someone else these days, but all he says is, What has that to do with anything?

Maybe I won't see him again. Grafton. It sometimes occurs to me that if I could be a lesbian it would solve everything. Well, not everything, but some things. Certainly I respect women more than I do men, feel closer to women, appreciate their beauty, have no fear of them as I do (secretly) of men . . . still it hasn't turned out that way. When it comes right down to it—bed—I really only want to be in one with a man. The more passion I bring out in him the more respect I have for myself, the more I appreciate my own beauty, whatever it may be. And yet a woman is a mirror I hold up, look into and question: Is that me?

I think I will see Jess after all. Claude said, why don't we go together? but I told him no, I'd rather go alone.

Jess

As Garnet sat on the sofa under the Tamara De Lempicka portrait of Dolores, time telescoped backward and I saw the child that I was, and finding her in the old familiar place, I gave a sigh of relief . . . no longer dispossessed, but home. As I moved about smiling foolishly, fumbling with the tea things, she made me aware in a way I hadn't been before that perhaps I too resemble my mother—a straight line of eyebrow, a look in the smile of the wide mouth. Still . . . I am fair-haired while Garnet is dark as Dolores is dark, dark as the enveloping night, and so the image of myself reflected in her slipped away. Not that I haven't thought of coloring my hair—oh, so often—but I am fair-haired in my mother's memory and should so remain until we meet again.

Then, suddenly, Katie ran into the room, saying, "Oh, Darling Ma—I was so afraid I'd be too late to meet Miss Blackburn." Perfect timing, I told her, and pushed back a tendril of the wild dark hair rippling around her face, for she'd rushed straight from rehearsal to meet Garnet: quite out of breath and still in her practice leotards. In them she always appears taller, more slender, with something otherworldly about her . . . a dragonfly touched by sunlight as it skims across the lake at daybreak. Her skin without make-up is translucent, lit from within. It is only on stage, when she dances, that to this delicacy character and strength are added—the dragonfly become woman. She kept doing her best not to stare at Garnet, who had moved over to the library table and picked up a silver-framed portrait, which she was looking at closely: Dolores in profile, photographed by Hurrell. Yes, Garnet would be drawn to that one, for in certain attitudes her face too is an exquisite star face camouflaged by lighting that obscures the person inside (if indeed there is a person inside to obscure). She put the photograph back on the table and went over to the ottoman, where I had piled several of the albums. She opened the first one and saw: Mr. and Mrs. Drew Willis, just returned from their honeymoon in Paris, attending Newport Cup Race . . . Dolores and Drew at a state dinner honoring King Alfonso of Spain . . . opening Metropolitan Opera . . .

Then she turned a page and suddenly there were no more of Dolores and Drew, only:

Dolores in billowing pajamas, white straw hat, hair waving around her shoulders, laughing, walking on a pebbly beach hand in hand between a man in a striped fisherman's jersey and a woman in a Moroccan caftan who pulls slightly away, gazing off at the sea. Underneath, scrawled in Dolores's hand: *End of Summer—La Garoupe, 1928—Charles Dana Gibson—Natasha Rambova*

Dolores, in front of a René Lalique fountain laughing with a woman holding a Pekingese under her arm and smoking a cigarette in a longer holder: *Duff Twysdens and Pooks the day we went to Versailles, Spring 1930*

Dolores in pleated skirt, wide-brimmed hat almost covering her eyes, sitting with Noel Coward holding a tennis racket: *June 1930—Lawn Tennis Tournament—Hanover Lodge, Regents Park*

Dolores entering the Champs Elysées Theatre with Rolf de Mare, Cole Porter; in the crowd, George Antheil with Josephine Baker.

Dolores as Queen Isabella with a costumed Christopher Columbus, greeting George Sand and Chopin: *Strauss Ball—Savoy Hotel, London—Gordon Selfridge, Ottoline and Philip Morrell*

Dolores conversing with Blaise Cendrars, with Marguerite de Bassians, Valéry, Harry and Caresse Crosby breaking into laughter: *Paris—Chez Josephine*

Dolores in sable against the snow, skaters in the distance, and under the photograph, white ink against the black page: *St. Moritz—the week before I met Nicolai*

Dolores, dark eyes gazing at a man opposite her—we see only his back. At a nearby table, a couple, the woman in black, the man—James Joyce? But who is it with Dolores? Thick-set, hands caught mid-gesture, he leans toward her—Nicolai? Underneath the photograph, nothing scrawled but: *Spring 1932—Paris—Trianon Restaurant*

Garnet put the album aside and I found myself saying, "Tell us about *your* mother."

"Well . . ." She smiled, spreading her hands out over the album and pressing down gently as if to put her mark on the leather. "My mother is . . . my mother. In appearance she's not a bit soignée in the way Dolores is—still she does unexpectedly chic things sometimes, like picking up a russet oak leaf in November and pinning it to her jacket. My mother and I are close, I suppose; certainly I'm closer to her than to my father, probably because of the way he treats her."

She stopped, regretted saying so much and stood up abruptly. "My—it's late! I must go."

Katie helped Garnet into her cape of crushed velvet and we stood watching her as she glanced in the hall mirror, folding the magenta silk lining around her, adjusting the hood just right over her blackberry hair. It had started to rain. But that didn't bother her and off she went, pausing to wave: "Good-bye, Katie. See you soon, Jess."

"Take good care," Katie called after her, but Garnet had already turned the corner.

"Well—what did you think?" I asked Katie.

"Ma, are you sure she isn't related to us?"

"Maybe in another life." I smiled and gave her a hug.

"Do you think I'll ever meet Dolores—do you really think after all this time that she's alive? Even if she is, she'll be so old . . ."

That is true—only, I never think of her that way. No matter how much time goes by, a part of me is back there when it happened, the day I woke and she wasn't there . . . Something seized my heart that day, held fast, and hasn't let go. That's why I've never given up hope, why I have all sorts of plans, things we'll do together when we do find each other, and at the top of my list is to take her to see Katie dance.

"Oh, Katie," I say now, "of course she's alive. We'll find her someday; she'll come to see you in *Giselle*—I really believe that."

"Then I do too, Mom. What fun it will be to know you're both out there loving and cheering me on."

You can't want something that much without making it happen.

Garnet

My mother is Madame Renoir, my father an elongated figure of El Greco, as withholding as my mother is giving. My mother is apricot and brown, my father blue: ice blue. Except to his girlfriend. I made that discovery unexpectedly one day quite early on, in Boston at the Isabella Stewart Gardner Museum, of all places. But why not? What better or more romantic place for a rendezvous, especially when you live in Philadelphia? Still at the time it was a shock, turned my father into someone I didn't know. By now, though, everyone in the family silently accepts the situation, this second marriage of his. Even my mother doesn't seem to mind anymore. It gives her time for herself. She just reread her treasured green leather edition of the Complete Works of Jane Austen, presented to her by my grandmother as a wedding present along with the family pearls. More than anything she loves to read and most often when she's not reading, her portable cassette player follows her into the greenhouse in winter, and in summer into the garden behind our house in Society Hill, where she listens to Proust while pruning the roses. But I'm not of so accepting a nature. I'm angry about the years it took him away from us: between that and his work—well . . . Now of course it's too late. We're grown up and it doesn't matter.

His girlfriend's name is Pepper Pearl. She went back to her maiden name when she divorced a Mr. Weedon and is now a cellist in the Philadelphia Orchestra. Actually, under different circumstances, we'd probably be friends. She bears a disturbing resemblance to my mother, although I am hard put to say just why, because she is flamboyant, the very opposite of my mother except in concerts, performing, when her hair is plaited in neat braids around her head and in her black dress she fades into the black-and-white ensemble of the orchestra in a most suitable manner. It's only offstage that she's peppery and pearly: bright dresses and charm bracelets, red raincoats and purple umbrellas to hold over her long bouncing red hair. I know these things because of my obsessive curiosity about her at one time, about the secret life she and my father had together. But no longer. Having settled into an accepting resentment, I don't dwell on their liaison. Philadelphia's a small town but there's room enough for all to live in peace. Or so it seems.

My father was in Boston for a series of lectures at Harvard and it was quite by chance that I came upon him and Pepper Pearl, although her name was of course unknown to me at the time. They were locked in an embrace in an alcove just inside the entrance to the Gothic Room. He had her pinioned against the wall, with one of her legs bent in pliant surrender as she cleaved to him. It was immediately clear that both had been carried away, as they say, and were in need of a bed. They didn't even notice me as I pulled back and ran down the three flights of stairs and into the street. All I wanted to do was get out of there as if I hadn't seen them. But the curve of her neck had burnt itself into my heart, the head limp against the wall, the swooning gesture as her hands first tried pushing him away and, then, the letting go. So I hurried back in again and spooked around the statues in Fenway Court, waiting for them to emerge, come down the steps, determined to get another look at her.

I tried to concentrate on the mosaic, the one on the floor in the center of the court. It's Roman, a Medusa, surrounded by scrolling vines and birds, but in place of Medusa's face I kept seeing *her* face, limpid and melting—her face as it had been when my father leaned close to her—and although it was peaceful there in the court among the displays of freesia, jasmine and azaleas, my poor heart wasn't calmed at all. They never did show up. Had I imagined it?

A month later I told my father I'd seen them.

"When you're older you'll understand," he said, with such authority and calm that I believed him. It was only after I'd put it out of my mind that I knew what he had said was true. I did understand. Only I never would. And I still don't.

Jess

Garnet hasn't called. The cape is something Dolores would have worn. Yes, the way the magenta silk framed her face would have suited Dolores very well indeed.

The Diaries of Dolores Willis

THE GORKY SANITARIUM

No, the blue Danube isn't blue isn't blue isn't blue it's a mustard soup and was I to Nico only a *Liebelei*, a bittersweet dalliance, or worse still—oh, God help me—a *Schmäh*? The maids in the Bristol Hotel kept smiling as they advised me to wait for the sunny day, the clear sunny day, that would appear—they do they do, though infrequently, the maids kept chirping, curtsying up and down. How were they to know I was onto them all along and knew that their organdy headdresses were really white butterflies which had alighted momentarily on their heads for a brief sojourn before moving on. Yes—they kept reassuring me—it is only on the sunny days that the Danube is blue; never on dull dreary gray days, so unwelcome on a pleasure trip. But the woods—ah! the Vienna Woods did not disappoint—as Nico and I walked along the melancholy promenades and later, in the hills near Heiligenstadt under a tree of white lilacs, leaves of green touched his dark hair as he leaned over me, and I reached up to push away the dew-laden branches, for the flowers, rich as grapes, the fresh white sweetness, made me faint, the scent with joy suffocated me.

One moment is all I ask—one moment to get away from this place. Could I not be taken back to the path we strayed upon that other dawn in the woods when we paused to rest on the moss? The cry that pierced the dawn . . . the nightingale's or mine?

Later we went to a tavern in the park to fox-trot under the trees—a diversion from the cabarets we had been frequenting. There were round tables and wicker chairs, chairs with arms to recline upon. I had worn the white gloves sprinkled with crystal stars presented to me by Dora Kallmus the week before Nico and I left for Vienna. However, he was too preoccupied that evening to fascinate. At the time I was annoyed, for serious though he was, he often could be diverted by my apparel, but now as I remember this, I shouldn't have been just annoyed, I

should have been really mad—yes, furious: that's so and anything else would be a lie. If only I'd paid more attention to the
talk around me: "Reds," "Blacks," "Blues," but how did I know
then that in their minds "Reds" = banners of red for Marxists,
"Blacks" = cassocks of black for Catholics; "Blues" = Bis-
marck's blue cornflower for the Pan-German nationalists; because at the time—fool that I was—these things drifted in and
out of my mind only as colors for a pretty dress. A certain shade
of blue is pleasant for me, but it must be pale, not too *foncée*;
lavender would be an even better choice to suit my fair skin,
so pale. In and out they drifted—the reds, the blacks, the blues,
in and out, but mostly out: little lodged there save thoughts of
Nico and how to amuse him in new ways so he wouldn't slip
away from me, which, now that I examine it, he was definitely
doing.

If only I'd paid more attention to Dora that day in her studio,
sighing in the lugubrious way she sometimes had, mumbling
about Vienna in 1933 being a far cry from the Wien she'd left
eight years before. Come to think of it—was it a warning? But
at the time I didn't give this a thought except to say, Ah,
Doruska, pet!—humoring her, believing her to be offering up
one of her mysterious innuendos, not unlike Mama's, which
had an irritating way of implying God knows what, a pouty
habit of hers I'd learned to overlook—and to divert her I pulled
on one of the gloves, twisting my slender hand in arabesques
for the stars to catch the sunlight, which streamed that day
through the skylight. "This must be recorded!" she said excit-
edly, quickly coming out of her melancholy, and soon she had
me doing God knows what in front of her camera, pirouetting
around in those damn white gloves, twinkle, twinkle—one of

her best fashion photographs, as it turned out: even Nico, so scoffing of Madame d'Ora's great gifts as a photographer, was speechless when he saw it and couldn't think of a word to say. But anyway, enough of that. It's those maids at the Bristol Hotel I keep worrying about—in and out they keep bobbing as bobolinks do, and as they bob out, back they bob in again. Then out again, on down the corridor and away, but just as I think that's that, back they come, twittering about the day we fox-trotted in the tavern, twittering about Nico and his turning away from me later in the Café Central with a look, paralyzing me with fear of what might come, and a foreboding possesses my being as it did then and I call out to him—Nico, prevent it, I beg you, helpless creatures—but I restrain myself from doing this, for you can bet it won't be Nico that comes out of the woodwork but one of the nurses who lurk in the hallways waiting for just such an event. It comes quickly to me how after we left the café and retired to our rooms the dreams started, but the screams stayed in my throat, silent, and in spasm—falling falling—paralysis came and I couldn't move from the bed in the Bristol Hotel. I was falling God knows into what darkness and I kept calling out to Nico even though I knew it was he who had dropped me down this well I spun around in, round and round spinning. Was it "the last straw" as dear Drew would say when I'd drawn Nico's attention to Dora's mise-en-scène photographs of the bloody pulp of helpless cattle, was it because I'd thrust these at him? His wrath did not frighten me that day—I wouldn't stop, beside myself as I was with this proof of the terror alive still in their dead eyes as it was in mine.

The hardness of him comes to me clearly for despite his love for me there was brutality, and I crack my head against it, and my heart breaks again, although how could it, for after that night the pieces were never put back together, or perhaps they were and the glue wasn't strong enough, or it was carelessly done, the placement of the pieces askew, slightly. If you know tell me, I beg you.

Yes, it was the slaughterhouses of Paris that Dora was intensely preoccupied with, but when it came right down to it any slaughterhouse would do. Hadn't she often spoken longingly of a future trip to Chicago, where they specialize in such horrors? How *could* you? I pleaded with her, but how could she know that the mere sight of a feather falling from a bird brings torment into a mind already overburdened with the pain inflicted on the poor dumb creatures of this world. "It is but a facet of my art," or something along those lines, she'd say wearily, as though explaining to a backward child. "My photographs of slaughtered animals state the impossibility of escaping death and decomposition and confront death bravely by presenting it as art." So much for that: what? Dead rabbits too she'd find daily in the refuse on the streets of Paris—those too were unspared, composed in front of her miserable camera in the name of art, and when I started weeping, out came her camera, but I said No! Absolutely not! No photographs! and fled her studio in fury, weeping, straight to Nico, who as usual wanted to hear none of it and so once again I was made to suffer alone.

Why was I drawn to this Dora woman, whose philosophy, so inhumane, so often destroyed my enjoyment of a pretty hat or a new dress? Was it because her still lifes of slaughtered animals, their chopped-off limbs and heads in shining blood puddles made real to me by abhorrence of the pain inflicted on innocents—these horrors were in such contrast to her photographs of fashion? How elegant they were, those other photographs of the women she adored—myself included; what style—our dresses, hats and jewels; how sensitive, dear Doruska, interpreting our uniqueness as no one else could.

These thoughts become as garlic on my fingers, for no matter how I try breathing it away, the deeper the breath I take the more the garlic seeps down into my skin, on into my veins, up into my brain and into the Café Central, into its corniced arches and chandeliers, globes of pale light high over the round tables where Nico and I sat with Alma Mahler and Kokoschka that night. How Alma had gone on about Klimt, boring me to death about his pursuing her to Venice, tracking her down finally in St. Mark's Square, where amid the crowds he bade her to abandon all and follow him—all quite annoying, but to Kokoshka most of all. He finally left in a stomp—bumping into a man coming into the café, some friend of Nico's as it turned out, one I hadn't met, the name eludes me but not, as so often happens, the face. Anyway, there we sat amusing ourselves. Alma had feet not larger than a rather large mouse, which were shod that night in gray alligator shoes, boots some might say, with pearl buttons going up one side, four in a row. How charming they were with their pointy toes; she had a certain way about her, I must admit. But why not—brought up as she was to so be. But then so was I. All Mama's and Papa's friends said I had the gift of innocence—they talked about me along those lines constantly—a gift Alma sadly lacked. It's this gift that's put me in this place, with the damn bobolinks from the Bristol Hotel and these pages as white as the white sheet I lie under.

.   .   .

I always knew how to please, but what good does it do me now? And speaking of *that*—I'd give a lot to know what time it is, what year, and what's going on right now at the Café Central. Black, no doubt, black and empty like the room here they sometimes put me in—the ceilings stripped of the chandeliers with golden globes I looked up into, globes of moonlight that floated above us that night as we lingered over our *mélanges*, with Alma making quite a fool of herself while I sat serene and silent, secure in Nico's love.

The Christian faction of the Soviet regime was a fact I tried to comprehend, but the ins and outs of governments had never been my forte and there I'd sit, pretty *poupée* that I was, doing my best to pick up bits and pieces here and there. One evening at Natalie's . . . Julian Huxley back that very day from his trip to Russia going on and on about how we must cast aside our preconceived views of the ideal society—something more or less along those lines. "Go! Go! Go!" he kept saying. "Go to Russia for inspiration." I'm all for that, I said, struggling to keep up my end of the conversation, but before I could get a word in edgewise he babbled on about the physique of the average man and woman in Russia, how far superior to that of the English. What about the Americans, Tarzan and so forth? I started to say, but Nico pressed my foot under the table quite hard and kept looking at me in that way he sometimes had, so I knew it was wiser not to get in deeper than I already was. From then on I just kept smiling a lot, and so in that way the evening passed.

Garnet

NEW YORK CITY

As I turned the corner and started down Lexington Avenue after leaving Jess's, the rain had turned to a wistful mist, but I could see a figure waiting in the distance outside Mortimer's and knew it was the faithful Claude. Can you imagine Grafton doing that, ever? He'd be sitting inside over his gimlet, one arm resting on the table, the other with a cigarette, musing over what might please him next. And when Claude and I sat down at our table—there he was, at the table next to us, with none other than Jane! They were in some kind of serious tête-à-tête, unaware of our arrival. Well, we were bound to run into each other sooner or later; still for a second I wanted to bolt, but how silly. What's the worst that could happen? Nothing but "hello." Of course I realize now that Grafton had spotted us as soon as we'd walked in; it's just his way to pretend he didn't—unlike Jane, who waved gleefully while Grafton, turning slightly, nodded our way, rather curtly. By then Claude was eagerly pressing for details about my meeting with Jess. And what of Dolores? What did I think of Dolores? For it's quite true, what he said—we do remarkably resemble each other. No wonder Jess is intrigued. But I don't want to get close to her— oh, a little maybe, but . . . maybe I'll grow my hair long, marcel the soft skeins in the fashion of Dolores, with a chignon loosely centered at the nape of the neck. Yes, something as banal as a new hairstyle is perhaps all I need to ease me out of this malaise.

Seeing Grafton and Jane entangles me again when I thought it was over. But I'll manage.

Just as I thought I was—managing, I mean—I ran into Jane quite by chance on Grove Street and we went into The Pink Teacup and had pecan pie with lots of whipped cream. Janey deserves better than Grafton. We both do.

Jane

Garnet's quite preoccupied in a way I've never seen her before. With her hair, mainly—usually she washes it every day in the shower, takes the drips off with a towel and it dries on its own right into shape. It's the cut, she keeps telling me whenever I envy her not having to fuss with rollers and teasing and the endless primping I go through. The cut! No, it's the hair—she has that Japanese kind of hair that just falls straight and oh well why waste time on wishing my hair wasn't a mass of cotton balls—it's all that bleaching I suppose, years and years of bleach bleach bleach. What the hell, I have other attributes she'll never have—attributes like—too many to go into right now. Anyway she's skipping her biweekly cut and letting it grow. All because of some fancy after meeting a friend of Claude's whose mother was a great beauty called Dolores Willis. She showed Garnet some photographs of her mother and Garnet's been quite mesmerized, so intrigued she's amusing herself by encouraging her hair to grow long like Dolores's. She refuses to talk much about it but I can tell she's even toying with the idea of dressing in a costumey way—thirties on-the-bias look. Why? I asked her. But she just smiled and said, "That's for me to know and you to find out." Can't you come up with a more original answer than that? I asked. "Oh come on, Janey, it's only make-believe," she said. So I let it go at that but don't think I wasn't on to her double entendre—still she's off tomorrow on a trip to Paris with Claude and I want our parting, though brief, to be on a cheery note. By the time you get back, I said, it'll be as long as Mother Dolores's. Thanks, she said, and that was that.

After Garnet left, it occurred to me I hadn't been in touch with my own little mother, Desirée, in quite a while. I'd called her when I arrived in New York, but we got into one of our hassles and I decided that this time I'd really had it with her and would save my energies for other performances. She's something, that woman, and I'm going to stick to my plan and not let her get to me this time round.

She was born in Hungary—need I say more? She does a big number about her baby—me—being born to her when she was only a baby—fourteen or so—but this could be fond illusion, because she improvises to suit herself as she goes along (don't we all). Well—anyway, she does look amazingly young, like my sister when we're together—you know, that kind of thing—so maybe there is only fourteen years between us. As to her parents, sometimes there are intimations of royalty in the background, other times it's money there somewhere, still other times she'll turn away to brush off a tear or two as if it's all too much for her to go into. Then she'll wander off onto other subjects, usually coming round to Simon Shemuel and how he made arrangements for me to be taken out of the orphanage. Desirée must have had a few qualms about that: it might complicate plans she had for herself and Mr. Shemuel, the path they were about to take down the road of life together. Still . . . fair's fair and she could have kept me a secret but she chose not to. Had she done so, I would have stayed on in the orphanage, my existence forever unbeknownst to Mr. Shemuel. As it turned out, he's the most loving man, the most generous-spirited, and from the moment he knew Desirée had a daughter he welcomed me into their lives as if I were his own. I've never known if she regrets the decision to reveal my existence or how she really feels about my being in the world. Some days I'm her "baby," other days it's "I should have flushed you down the toilet." But I'm used to her way of putting things and by now our fights and reconciliations have become a recurrent theme in our ongoing mutual enthrallment. Mr. Shemuel was pretty enthralled too, although he gave up long ago, and I'm still hanging in there. Well, she can be Dolly Adorable when it behooves her, and Dolly Adorable she was right up until the day she and Mr. Shemuel were married. After, it was back to her old self again, that self I know and love. But it didn't seem to make any difference, because Mr. Shemuel went right on adoring her for years and years and years. Much as I love him and think of him as my father, I still keep trying to find out from Desirée who my real father is. But she won't tell me. Does she know?

Anyway, when Mr. Shemuel married my mother he adopted me and I was no longer Marygold No-One-on-Earth, I was Miss Marygold Shemuel. I called him Daddy, but my mother kept on referring to him as Mr. Shemuel. One of her affectations, no doubt.

The wedding took place in London just before the outbreak of the war, and soon after, I flew with my mother and Daddy across the ocean to New York City. There we lived in a big place on the top floor of the Hampshire House, overlooking Central Park.

My room had pink cabbage roses on the walls going right up over the ceiling, and the pink carpeting was soft as moss roses when I walked into the room. Over my bed there was a dotted swiss canopy and under it sheets sprinkled with roses, roses too on the downy pillows, which were filled with feathers, each and every one plucked by hand from a real goose. They were so squashy I needed two, sometimes three, under my head to feel just right. Rose vines trailed over the table by my bed, specially painted to go with the wallpaper. On it stood a bouquet of pink tea roses bunched together with a lace ruffle and pink bows. It looked like a real old-fashioned bouquet but it was made of china. Tea roses were sprinkled on the pink lampshade to cast a rosy glow around my bed when night came. Now this sounds like too much rosy pink, I know, but it was pluperfect, I can tell you!

Whenever I could maneuver it I'd follow my mother through the apartment as she showed it off to her friends. "Decorated by Dorothy Draper," she'd always say, adding modestly, " . . . well, with lots of help from Desirée, of course."

I had more toys than the windows of F.A.O. Schwarz, but the only thing I really wanted was my mother's undivided attention. To get this I started acting. Honestly I can't recall a time when I wasn't playacting in one way or another. Happy acting or needy acting or whatever acting it took. There was no end to the inventiveness of my repertoire, and as I grew up refinements were added—a touch here, a touch there, but the main touch had to do with truth, real truth, because eventually the borderlines wove in and out so skillfully there was no difference between one and the other.

Isn't Marygold a pretty name? I really like that name, which belongs to me. Of course I could have kept it for stage purposes, and I almost did but decided not to because it's not a serious name. There are some names like that—Gigi names, which only work if you're sixteen and living in Paris. Marygold is serious only if you come across it in a fairy tale. But the name I made up—Jane Esmond—is serious, isn't it? I thought Daddy might be upset by my not being Marygold Shemuel anymore, but he said, "Darlin', you'll always be my girl no matter what you call yourself."

As for Desirée . . .

"Actress! Whatever gave her that idea?"

That's what she said.

When we lived at the Hampshire House, my mother had a bathroom as big as her bedroom, but it looked even bigger because everything was mirrored, even the ceiling. On one entire wall there were mirrored shelves where she kept bottles of perfume: Chypre, My Sin, Shalimar, Vol De Nuit, on and on, row on row, each in a different and more diverting bottle than the one next to it. But she never opened any of them, because they were just there for show, except for one flacon on her dressing table. It contained perfume of a pale taffy color the exact shade of her hair, and from the crystal stopper there dangled a silken taffy tassel. I used to sneak into her bathroom when she wasn't there just to close my eyes and touch it, because it reminded me of the times my mother hugged me and her silken taffy hair would swing across my cheek. Le Tabac Blond, it was called, and it was the only scent she lavished on herself except for the lotions and bath salts that were placed around the edge of her tub. One was a jar filled with Bluegrass, and the other was Mimosa—crystals luscious as rock candy, aqua and yellow, to perfume her bath. "I'm ready for my bath now," she'd say to the maid, and the maid would tiptoe about, turning on faucets and laying out my mother's terry robe on the little chair by the tub.

After these matters were attended to she usually waved the maid away, for there were some things she enjoyed doing for herself, such as dipping her long lacquered fingernails into the jars of salts, scooping out a handful of aqua or yellow or mixing them together, depending on her mood. Extravagantly the rock candy would be scattered down under the hot water plunging from the golden dolphin faucet into the milky marble of the tub, while she leaned over, trailing a washcloth to and fro so the chips of blue or yellow would melt faster and singing to herself in the sweetest of voices, "My life a wreck you're ma-king, you know I'm yours for just the ta-king, I gladly surren-der—myself to you, bod-eee and soul." Hanging up over the tub on a golden hook was a frilly lace-trimmed baby pillowcase, at least that's what it looked like. It was made of charmeuse— "not beige, baby, not beige," my mother'd say, "French nude." She was referring to its color, which was carried over into her boudoir dresses, camisoles and so on, right down to flossy pom-poms on her French nude slippers. And why not, for no shade was more suited to her tawny beauty. Anyway—to get back to the baby pillowcase—in the center of it were satiny flowers fashioning a *D*, for Desirée, naturally, and it hung there over the tub on a silken cord with a golden tassel, the prettiest thing you ever saw. Inside was my mother's rubber douche bag, which she used every day just before Daddy arrived, as he always did, promptly at two o'clock from his office. That's why my mother's lunch dates, when she had them, were always brunches instead of lunches. She had to be home and ready for Mr. Shemuel, because he came back from his office to make love to her every day at two o'clock on the dot. Of course my mother never confided these things to me, but I found out about them one way or another. Children always do.

When my mother got pregnant, she was her very most impossible self. Complaining, complaining all the time, especially toward the end, when she wouldn't set foot out of her room or see any of her friends but lay about all day on a chaise longue, jiggling at the quartz bell for the maid to hurry in and do her bidding. On the table beside her there'd be a lavender tin box of Louis Sherry licorice cats and next to it another box from Louis Sherry, quilted in lavender satin. She'd open it, perusing the rows of chocolate shapes filled with orange creme, caramel, or perhaps a strawberry, hard put to decide which to take, saying to the maid, do this or that, complaining, complaining.

"At least it'll be a boy!" she'd sigh, leaning back on the lacy pillows and turning to gaze out at the snow falling over Central Park.

After this prophecy she'd pick up the enameled hand mirror from her lap, holding it at arm's length. It gave her a pretty good reflection of herself as she lay there, and after a while there'd be another sigh.

"Think of it, buttercup. A boy!"

This consoled her, momentarily, for the "disfigurement," as she called it, which just had to be put up with a while longer. Reassured, she'd hand me the mirror to put back on the table next to the licorice cats.

"Pull down the shades, babykins," she'd say, and once I had, off she'd drift into her nap.

Mr. Shemuel was a veritable saint throughout these months. No more home-on-the-dot-of-two-each-day—it was home at the end of the day, with presents. Full of high hopes, he'd bound in not only with red-and-gold tooled-leather boxes from Cartier but with silly loving presents meant to make her laugh.

His efforts received the vaguest of thanks and the weakest of smiles, however, and why he put up with her or kept coming back for more is a subject to speculate upon. But come back he did, each time with a more tempting surprise, at his wits' end trying, trying to please her and take her mind off the dreary days she must endure. Not that she didn't want it, this baby. She did. To cement the situation, no doubt . . .

Then she gave birth—to a perfect rosebud of a baby girl instead of the boy she'd been counting on.

"Was I that pretty?" I asked, gazing down into the bassinet in wonder at my infant sister. But my mother only sighed and sighed, saying, "The mirror, baby, hand me my mirror," and when I did she turned this way and that, examining her face, quite desolate, as though the secret of the universe had been lost, when in truth she looked more beautiful than ever.

"Baby's the image of you, my darlin'," Mr. Shemuel would whisper, leaning over and kissing my mother—oh, so tenderly—on her forehead, then on her eyes, her cheeks, her nose, her mouth. Oh, how he did dote on her!

"We'll name her Desirée after you—she'll be my little Desirée."

"Little Desirée!" My mother was appalled by that idea. "No—not little Desirée at all! Little something or other . . . I don't know what, but"—she wiggled her fingers in baby's direction—"but I'll think of something."

Mr. Shemuel just smiled and put it all down to those "baby blues" he'd heard mothers get after the agonies of birth-giving. A few days' rest and she'd have another point of view, a change of heart, he thought. But she didn't. I could have told him she wouldn't. Still, wisely, I stayed out of it, awaiting developments, which just might portend her turning some of her attention on me—it was a long shot, but I kept hoping.

"You've met my baby." My mother waved toward me as friends piled in to see the new arrival. She was recuperating from the birth, reclining once more on the chaise longue, with Mr. Shemuel's latest offering—an ermine lap robe—draped over her. Tails of ermines had been sewn in a border around the edges, and now and again she'd pull at them, twirling them in the most distracting way, never glancing over at the real little baby girl in her inappropriate blue-ribboned bassinet, with a nanny in attendance. She was English, this nanny, but then they all were, because soon we were to move back to London, to a house Mr. Shemuel had bought on Chester Square.

How they came and went, those nannies, though that wasn't because of my mother's impossible nature. If it had been up to her, things would have slid along their natural course, with the nannies doing it their way, which is what English nannies want most, do best and in fact insist on. No, it was Mr. Shemuel who caused the parade of nannies to troop in and out one week after another. He doted on his baby daughter, and it was doubtful if there was a nanny born who would ever please him or be perfect enough to tend his rose baby. That's what he called her—Rosebaby. When my mother nixed Desirée, he said her name would be Rosemary, because she was his baby rose, and even though my mother had a fit and said, "Nonsense! It will be Sondra, because Sondra has more chic," still he stood firm, and finally she lost interest and gave in. "Oh, all right, Rosemarie then."

"No—*Rosemary*," he said, and so it was.

Right up to this day Daddy still calls Rosemary "Rosebaby." But he loves me more, even though I'm adopted and Rosemary's his own—things like that you can feel—and when I realized this was true it was like fitting a tiny piece of puzzle way up somewhere in the corner of the big puzzle and for a moment, from somewhere inside, came a quiver from someone or other, a glimmer of something or other—satisfaction maybe.

But such moments don't last. When it comes right down to it, no matter how hard I tap-dance, things are always more or less the same. Still, it's those glimmers that keep me moving, because the better the performance the more the applause: that's the glimmer part, and when that's over there's the next time—maybe. It's the times between the glimmers that I don't know what to do with. Oh well.

Tap-dancing is what it's about. Early on I made that discovery, and if my mother lies about everything, I do it better. I'm more imaginative than Desirée, brighter certainly, and even with my mask of toughness there's the unexpected mask of my vulnerability on call to take over if the situation demands. Desirée's too contrived to have credibility; even on a stage it wouldn't work, not really—much too fancy-built. But maybe that's because I'm a professional and notice such things. Others fall for it—men, that is; of course women usually catch on to her right away. That's why she has so few women friends. Actually, I can't think of one. So on both counts, off stage and on, we're talking about talent, aren't we, and when it comes to projecting the big lie, I do it better. Because I start believing, and when that happens it isn't a lie anymore. It's truth. That's what truth is, isn't it? It's what you believe.

Leaving out my technical skills, which are damn good, that's why I'm a star. "Believe it, kid," is all the direction the director gave me on my first movie before he started the scene rolling. It gave me pause. There's a lot to be said for those three little words. And that's what I do. No dinkum oil from this one. I believe the make-believe. But Desirée doesn't. She's shrewd, all right, but not intuitive enough to forget it's a lie.

Desirée enchanted herself with the divertissements at the house on Chester Square. Parties every day, it seemed. Mr. Shemuel had other things on his mind, traveling on business, but it amused him to indulge my mother and know she was enjoying herself even if he had to be away. He didn't even seem to mind her flirtations with the men, married or otherwise, who came to her lunches and soireés, nor for years did he cease to be captivated by her need to bedizen and bedeck her Dolly Adorable Self. Yes, she's a real doll, as they say, although in my view she's more of a bantamweight boxer. Still I can see how she appeared to a man—fun to play with yet not be fearful of breaking, because behind her pliant and giving manner, deceptive though it might be, there was the open invitation suggesting an energy and a vitality worth lusting after. Who would guess that the one thing on her mind was the pampering and titivating of herself? Ah! Desirée, with your eyes of cinnamon and your lids grazed with topaz shadow and your nose—rather too large—so skillfully shaded with loving handiwork to present a more pleasing delicacy, and as for the delectable mouth . . . how quick it was to smile. How edited she was in every way, right down to the scripts—the starring vehicles she devised for herself with an uncanny way of hitting on just the right scene to vamp the man of the moment into believing she lived only to satisfy his heart's desire. I learned a lot just watching her, and even though her little ways wouldn't hold up on a stage, I sometimes use them to experiment with in rehearsal when I'm working on a part.

"Tell me," I once naively asked her, "what do you lie about? To a man, I mean."

"Oh, Pussycat—everything!" She laughed.

"I *worked* for what I got!" she says now. She means the settlement—hefty—Daddy gave her when he finally divorced her, along with the things he had given her before that: the house in Chester Square with its Colefax & Fowler decorations, the accoutrements that went with it, the Paris dresses; but most of all the money. That's what really catches her interest—she's always been a collector of silver and gold and dollars. Serious jewels also acceptable. As for the "work" part of it—that's her description of her years with Simon Shemuel—well, I suppose it is a strain pretending all the time. It's not like playing to a vast breathing mass out there somewhere that you can feel but not see: there's more pressure when you're playing to an audience of one. Of course for a real actress it's already part of the territory.

After the divorce she sold the house on Chester Square and put her loot into a Swiss bank account before moving back to New York. There she settled into a two-room rent-controlled apartment on West Eighty-sixth where she still lives. It's comfortable enough, with its plastic-slipcovered furniture and kitchenette. On the shelf over the basin of the small bathroom is a flacon of Le Tabac Blond, and unopened though it may be in its gold-and-beige box, it has its memories. She's become reclusive, although she always makes the effort to see me if I happen to be in a play in New York. I keep trying to get her to London, but travel costs too much and even if I suggest the trip as a present from me she declines. It's a relief when she does, because one way or another, when we do see each other we always end up in a fight. Now and again, to cheer her, I'll send flowers, but it's always the same.

"Don't send flowers," she screams over the phone. "Send me the cash instead."

Time passes, however, and I forget and keep on sending flowers instead of the money I spend on them, and she keeps on with the screaming, and round and round it goes. The matter could easily be resolved by my doing as she asks. But I don't. Well—finally we all do what we really want to be doing. At least so I've heard.

On stage is the only place where I feel O.K.—you know, safe. Oh, in front of the camera too, of course. Forget the rest—they're only places I visit before I go back home. What'll happen? Where will I live when the world grows dark and I am old and there are no more parts for me to play? Boo-hoo.

Garnet

PARIS

Dearly as I love Janey, lately she's been driving me up the wall with her probing, going on and on about the most inconsequential things. This trip to Paris with Claude is perfect timing although it wasn't so planned. When I get back she'll have forgotten I ever mentioned Jess's mother. Besides, I'll have a surprise for her—my hair will be cut again in the usual style. "It's much more becoming that way," she'll say triumphantly. "What is?" I'll say, as if I didn't know what she was talking about. Jane will believe I've forgotten about Dolores, but of course I haven't. Every day here I keep thinking about her more than ever, imagining her in places Claude and I visit. Once I caught a glimpse of a woman in black with a silver fox boa and a veil—mesh pinned back with a diamond arrow—hurrying through the revolving Vendôme doors of the Ritz Hotel, late for a rendezvous. I was so sure it was Dolores I ran from Claude to follow her, but she turned the corner of the long passageway leading to the rue Cambon and when I caught up—she'd disappeared, vanished as if I'd dreamed it all. Yes, we have quite a relationship, Dolores and I, a bond—definitely. I wonder what she was like. What she is like now if she's alive and whether if I met her I would discover things about myself I hadn't ever thought of. And if I did—would it make a difference? A difference in the way I feel about even the important things? Or would I discover that she and I are not unlike at all, on the contrary—that there was nothing we didn't already know and recognize in each other, that there would be nothing to change, nothing to do, but to go on as I am.

The Diaries of Dolores Willis

THE GORKY SANITARIUM

Until I met Nicolai I never gave politics a thought. Everyone made a fuss over me and thought me beautiful, but I never gave much thought to that either. Whatever I had, worked, and I breathed at ease in the skin I was born in.

My mother, Amalia Figueroa, was—well, how can I say? Maybe another time; it's a long story. Anyway, Mama and Papa were always bickering and separating for one reason or another, and it was during one of these upsets, timed just at the outbreak of the War, that some other sort of upset was going on to over-throw the Menocal government in Cuba, and Papa was sent to Havana to report on the hysterics of the country, well versed as he was in dealing with those of Mama. We were in New York at the time, but the day after he left, Mama went even battier than she had been before—couldn't stand another min-ute without him, and to get me safely out of the way she started babbling about putting me in the school of the Convent of the Sacred Heart. Nico, I didn't take to this idea one bit. She said Papa didn't want me in Cuba, which I didn't believe for one second, but being still considered a child, what could I do except fume as I listened to her ramblings about how happy she'd been as a girl in the very same convent I was about to be exiled to and how I'd have the time of my life there. Ha ha! What kind of fool did she take me for? I'm no slouch myself when it comes to *grande hystérie*, having learned the basics at Mama's knee— a certain way she had of drawing her lips tighter and tighter into a thin line, making them disappear into her face in a most disturbing manner. So I took a deep breath and made one hell of a scene, I can tell you, but Mama won out in the end as she always did. From the outside, that prison—I mean that convent looked like a prison. When the door opened, however, a nun answered sweetly enough and said to follow her, the Reverend Mother Rallet was expecting us. Rallet rhymed with Mallet: a mallet to make me toe the line, *n'est-ce pas*, Nico? But what to do but follow the sweet-voiced one? And follow her we did, down corridors with stone floors smooth as pumice, past statues of saints in niches with red votive candles flickering at their feet and making pink shadows on their pearly marble toes. I got quite caught up in the peace of it all, the quiet being such a welcome change from the razzmatazz of life with Mama. Still I kept a sad face on, hoping to further upset her as around and up we went, until there, at the top of the stairs, a fatty figure in black held her arms out to me the way saints do in drawings on religious cards. Whether this fatty person was man or woman was anybody's guess, and even when we got closer I wasn't sure, but soon of course I knew it was Mother Rallet, so it must be a woman. Still . . .

Anyway, Mama couldn't wait to get out of there and said quickly, "Reverend Mother, I leave Dolores in your hands." Then she skiddooed back on down the stairs—faster than we'd come up, if you really want to know.

When Christmas came I kept telling myself I didn't really care about not being with Mama and Papa in Havana, because I was sent to visit with Priscilla Lanning, one of my schoolmates, who lived with her aunt, a Madame DeBrière, in a house on Fifth Avenue facing the Metropolitan Museum—like one of Ludwig's castles it was, not Neuschwanstein, one of the others. There was a ballroom with tapestries of beasts and maidens, and a chandelier of diamonds and emeralds floating from a sky of frescoed clouds. The Christmas tree was placed so that the pine branches reached up and intertwined with the chandelier's crystal branches and prisms—who could tell where one ended and the other began? I was told to call Madame DeBrière Auntie Nana, the way Priscilla did, and having no children of her own, she showered us with presents, finery and surprises. Snow kept falling falling all around the big house, and the trees in Central Park were laden with the fluffiness of it. I'd never seen so much snow, goo-foo feathers from heaven—it kept falling, turning everything into something it wasn't. Then the holidays were over and when I got back to the convent, a letter from Mama was waiting, saying come to Havana at the end of the spring term. I couldn't wait, because even though at the convent I'd been peaceful and happier than I'd ever been at home, it just wasn't the same.

That was some summer, Nico, that summer in Cuba, hot I can tell you, bougainvillea on hot-pink stucco houses, and afternoons floating around with this boy I'd met, Rufino—who come to think of it reminds me of you—in the hot waters of the Caribbean, eating sticky, dripping mangoes. Later he taught me the *danzón*, a dance where you stand very still gazing at each other and every once in a while as you move to the music you face a different direction. Sounds monotonous, but believe me, it's sexy as all get-out. Then everything got cloudy between Papa and Mama and they pushed me away again into that dark cave where I couldn't see, could only hear their never-ceasing voices. Even at night when they shut the doors to muffle the sounds and thought I didn't hear—I did and I was certain I was to go back to the convent, but then came a calm and I was told I'd only have to go back for a little while, for Papa was to be stationed in Brussels and when he and Mama were settled there they'd send for me.

Papa had a sweet tooth and liked chocolate with cherries inside: sticky brandy trickled over his chin when Mama popped one into his mouth and he'd bite into it, making us all laugh. Eventually, Mama's rages over his contessa friends faded away somewhere. He was exhausted by then. I could tell. So they stayed together.

Mama had a real thing against the Germans, due to some ancient drama about Papa and a diva he'd been most attentive

to in Munich—God knows when. Anyway, Mama hadn't forgiven the bestial Hun, so when he was appointed consul general
to Germany—this was long before Cuba, Nico—she tightened
her lips and flatly refused to accompany him to Hamburg. He
pleaded with her to go but she would have none of it, and off
he went alone while we held the fort in Barcelona. Letters came
from him every day and Mama pounced on each one for signs
and portents. Of particular interest was mention of any festivities in Hamburg, which she interpreted in her own way. Some
parts she'd read aloud; other parts not. The not parts infuriated
her. She'd roll her eyes around, muttering, "Orgies, orgies," and
although I was only a child, I knew that whatever *that* meant,
Papa was up to something. But I had to be satisfied with what
was forthcoming, and there's one particular letter that keeps
coming back to me, about an evening of gaiety at Kiel on Albert
Ballin's yacht. He was the president of the Hamburg-American
Line and this yachting party was in honor of the German emperor. The thing that sticks in my mind is a specially constructed
knife and fork the Emperor's valet brought on board for the Emperor's use, due to His Highness's short right arm, which had to
rest on the table throughout the banquet. Papa didn't go into
the manner in which this cutlery was dealt with, and I puzzled
then, as I do now, over the details of His Majesty's melancholy
predicament. Did the valet discreetly position the dining utensils in the Emperor's inert hand so the royal head could dip up
and down, birdlike, to partake of delicacies presented? Or were
they brandished with finesse by the royal left arm, while the
shorter one rested on the napery? Surely the latter.

Later, word came to us that Papa had been attending the
derby at the Hamburg race track when news broke of the Grand
Duke of Austria's assassination at Sarajevo. This news upset
Mama even more than the "orgies"—something was going to

happen, something terrible, like WAR maybe. It meant little to me at the time, high-strung child that I was, unduly wrought up by the Emperor's plight, still trying to figure out of what ingenious design was this singular cutlery. And was it gold? Surely yes.

Oh, Nico, did I tell you about Papa in 1919? He'd been appointed by President Wilson to take over the work of some commission in Belgium and I went there with them. Mama met me in Paris with Wexler and another aide of Papa's and we drove by motor to Belgium. Usually the trip took eight hours, but that time it took days and days because the roads through battlefields and open trenches were so bumpity-umpity we had to sit on the floor of the motor to avoid being thrown out. Mama was in hysterics most of the time and when night came we slept on pillows in the car because all around the houses were in ruins. There was no water, there was nothing. On the second day I slipped out into the dawn before Mama and the others were awake. The light was unearthly. In the distance an abandoned army tank jutted up against the horizon and I made my way toward it through the litter of rusted helmets and stumps of wood where trees had been, through the flat silence where no bird sang. I went up to the tank and stood on tiptoe to peer inside. But something grabbed my hand, taking the breath out of me as I struggled to pull away, then just as suddenly it was let go and I fell back on the ground and, jack-in-the-box-like, up popped an English tommy. "All you Americans pinching our stuff—how's this for a souvenir?" he said. And he thrust the skeleton of a blown-off hand into my face laughing. "Belong to your daddy maybe?"

.   .   .

The Belgian girls had short hair, not by choice but to brand them for doing they-wouldn't-tell-me-what with a German during the occupation. They stood out like freaks in a circus—pinheads, Nico, pinheads! How fragile their skulls, like those of sugar on Mexican graves on All Souls' Eve—easily cracked, you know what I mean. But there were pretty things to take my mind off them—flour bags sent from America stamped with a big American eagle, which the Belgians had taken and embroidered, embossing the eagle with silks of the most ravishing hues, to sell in Brussels. Papa gave one to Edith Cavell a week before she faced the firing squad—it was still on the wall of her room in the nursing home where she had been directress when she died. I'd like to hang it on the wall of my room right now to show these pinhead nurses a thing or two—*n'est-ce pas*, Nico?

Mama repeated herself so often that I stopped paying attention. Everybody wants something from you be warned There's no such thing as friendship because friends always want something Never give anything without a return patati pattata talk talk talk. Still . . . well, she was my mother, she knew more than I did. Maybe she was right.

Garnet

NEW YORK CITY

I keep thinking of Jess's daughter, Katie. Something about her . . . Of course, she too resembles her grandmother, Dolores—probably it's that.

I used to want a child, but you have to extend yourself, and Grafton's much too self-absorbed for that. "Oh, maybe I'll have a child when I'm eighty," he says cavalierly, going on with: "When I was fourteen my mother sent me to the right analyst, a woman, who encouraged me to do it my way, so my life's well planned."

There's no answer to that. As for Garnet Blackburn—her life isn't planned at all. All these years locked into Grafton, and I can't seem to move on. Before Grafton I was on guard, loath to trust, so it became a game: Who's going to win? This put an edge on things. Made even the slightest occurrence a contest. A contest nobody won. The seesaw went up and down, up and down. There was no end to it, up and down. Then the seesaw was locked in place. Grafton got me high up in the sky, quite pleased with himself—and although I know in my head there are no victims, only volunteers, he won't let me come down.

But—getting back to being responsible for another human being. I suppose that's what love means—being necessary to another person, responsible for his happiness. And that's not independence. Independence is when you can support yourself and when you're not afraid of being alone. I can say yes to that on both counts, finally. Still I ache sometimes for a singular attention Grafton is incapable of giving. An attention Claude is capable of giving but a responsibility I'm not sure I want— that is, from him. Grafton's going to change, I keep thinking, but of course he's not, and if he did, perhaps he wouldn't interest me and then I'd be free.

The Diaries of Dolores Willis

THE GORKY SANITARIUM

I have a daughter somewhere, at least I think I have. Why isn't she doing something about all this? Jessica something-or-other is her name and I wonder what she's up to these days. Good question, isn't it? I can't remember if her eyes are blue or brown . . . Anyway, that has nothing to do with Friedrich. He was the man whose name I couldn't think of, the one who came into the café that last night in Vienna, bumping into Kokoschka as he stomped out. His father had murdered some prime minister, over some political upset I never got the gist of; anyway, it wasn't the murderer who came into the café but the son of the murderer—in he came and over to our table, which brings me to recall, God knows why, a day in spring when I was happy. I was in a forest green walking by a stream, alone. It was before I met Nico—long before—and I didn't have to please anyone. The sunlight came through the trees, splashing on the leaves like rain, soundless sun-rain, patterning and pattering down, over me the light. I reached up but it flew away or was it the birds who clustered on branches above me, green birds flying up into the sun through the tall trees. Nothing seems real to me now save that, and what Friedrich Adler has to do with it I don't know.

A revolutionary upheaval took place in twenty-five million households, decided and carried through by government, the grain crisis of the winter of 1927–28, heralding the general crisis in NEP, the onset of collectivization, which happened during the winter of 1929–30. What did it mean? It had to do with Nicolai but all that comes to me is the erratic behavior of Mama after the Sarajevo incident . . . and that cutlery: Fabergé perhaps? I still haven't been able to picture it.

"Kulak" did not in the beginning have a negative meaning. It simply meant the better-off members of communes. Kulaks were strong, hardworking, efficient peasants who excelled in cultivating their land. Of course, speaking of that, I was instructed by Mama to cultivate only those I could get a return from. It was Nico who boasted of these other cultivations—boasted that between 1906 and 1916 the kulaks were great achievers in agricultural productivity, more so than the communal peasants or the *pomeshchiki*, whoever they were. Nico told me, but I forget.

Yes, the kulaks were a group whom the reformers—one in particular, Stolypin—expected to establish as a wealthy class without damaging the interests of the *pomeshchiki* and that section of the peasantry known as the *serednyaks*—the middle peasants if I remember correctly. Oh, Nicolai—where are you now to help me keep tabs on such matters? Stolypin was out of it, though, by 1911, something unexplainable happened to him (Nico became vague when pressed for details)—anyway, this Stolypin, whoever he was, never lived to see the results of what were known as the "Stolypin reforms." He must have been quite a card, that one, notorious for ruling by executive decree and taking decisive measures to prevent revolutionary goings-on in the provinces. Special court-martials were most necessary, Nico said, to carry out the thousand death sentences, maybe more, in 1907. Imagine! my birth year. And Nico's only a few years before. *Quelle coïncidence!* But it was all for the cause, whatever this Stolypin person did, and after all, Nico was only an infant—isn't that what I said? so was I—so no one could accuse him of being responsible in any way; nor me for that matter.

Barcelona!

I sit between Mama and Papa in my dress sky blue. The corrida is about to begin . . .

Below us in the arena, matadors, toreadors, banderilleros wait for the president to toss the key up up into the sun. Olé Olé roars the crowd before settling down to watch the spectacle.

Lace of softness melts into Mama's face, Grandmother Figueroa's mantilla held by comb of tortoiseshell, roses red tucked beneath. Ruffles of red silk, her fan tapping Papa's arm as she looks up into his eyes.

Throughout the arena, around us ruffling fans, thousands, but none with the beauty of Mama's agitated wings of kingfishers pounding my heart into rhythms of the *paso doble—*

My first corrida!

> The great sound
> The blood
> The bull

Biggest best of the day so far

to be fought in honor of our distinguished guest Sir Thomas Lipton beside Mama sitting . . .

For such triumph the matador superb awards the ears of the bull to the lady of his choice, but not today. Today they are bestowed on Sir Thomas, our distinguished guest, and still so still I sit as the matador stands in front of our seats bowing—bloody ears, reeking blood oh so tenderly held in the fold of

his red satin cape, so proudly, Mama smiling, her dress now
red as blood. Onto my dress it broke my bleeding heart.
  Olé Olé
  Sir Thomas rises, bowing.
  How graciously accepting the jubilation of blood
  Blood cattle dying from lack of fodder
  Kulaks dragging bloodless blue legs swollen from dropsy

Nicolai Nicolai you are not my mother

Jess

AMAGANSETT

It is weeks since it happened. I'm staying with friends in their
house on the beach where they live all year round though few
do for most leave after summer's end. Through the night the
winter surf comes to me, cold and chill, as I lie staring at the
darkened window of my room. Before dawn the sea shifts, the
sky settles down into it, dark as a lake, and as deep.

Down the road, also on the dunes, is the house Abe and I
rented the summer we were so happy, the summer Katie was
six. Her room was on the second floor next to ours, a corner
room, and just as the sun is setting I slip away down the road
and stand across the street staring at the deserted house. I stand
there as the clouds streaked with sun disappear, and as the sky
darkens, Katie appears in the window and sees me standing
across the road in the gathering dusk and she calls out:

"Daddy, come look! Who is that woman standing across the road?"

I start toward the house but the window is empty and I see her running out of the house, the familiar bang of the screen door is sharp in the crisp air, on down the steps she runs toward me in the darkening light, calling out:

"Darling Ma . . ."

The week before it happened the phone rang and it was Mac.

"I have to talk to you," he said.

"No," I said.

"Look—I've got to talk to you."

"There's nothing to say."

And there wasn't. I'd made up my mind, and this time I meant it. Really.

A few days later he called again.

"You know I love you. I miss you something awful—please, please."

He sounded desperate, and I too, so I said:

"Yes."

We were to meet in a restaurant but I'd left two hours earlier because Katie and I had planned that morning to go after her rehearsal to have ice cream in the place next door. The following night she was to debut with Baryshnikov and she'd been so busy I hadn't seen her in days. I got to Lincoln Center and she was already waiting outside and when she saw me she ran toward me as if with great news, something to tell me, something so exciting she couldn't wait for the light to change. She was running toward me across the street and as it started hap-

pening I was outside myself seeing it from a distance, far away
. . . What small figures we were among the traffic and crowds—
Katie in a red coat running toward me against the red light as
I shouted:

"Go back! Go back!"

The car hitting her full on, her face—an instant—it's not
bad, it's going to be all right—but she fell reaching her hand
out to me as the wheel crushed her head.

Garnet

NEW YORK CITY

Jane returned my call. "I'm finally back from Paris," I said.
"You won't recognize me."

"It's hard for me to make dates ahead," she said vaguely.
"Rehearsals, and then . . . the nights. You know how it is."

"Jane, tell me, why do you put up with Grafton?"

"What a question. I never think about why—I just do." She
laughed. "What about you?"

"Oh, I don't!"

"Umm . . ." she hummed. "Well!"

"Well, I don't! I have no interest in Grafton anymore."

"How about Saturday?" she said.

"I have new paintings you might like to see, paintings of
you."

"Oooo, lovely! Four o'clock I'll be there."

She was late, but I expected that. No make-up except a
touch of Vaseline under the eyes, quite breathless over tardiness
due to an irresistible amber kitten she'd seen in a pet shop

window. On the way, the creature had nestled down in the pocket of her polo coat and fallen asleep.

"Are you sure it's all right?" I asked.

She looked down at the tiny head, lolling over the edge of her pocket.

"It's not dead, is it!" Frightened, she touched the doleful chin, and the cat opened its eyes, stared at her, yawned and collapsed back into lethargy.

"Garnet, you can't imagine—the dear was frantic! Tap-tap-tapping on the glass—desperately—beckoning with her other little paw for me to get her out. I just couldn't walk away. What shall I call her?"

"That's going to take a lot of thought. In the meantime let me spread your coat out in the bedroom without disturbing her and make tea, or would you rather something else? Soave perhaps?

"Lovely!"

She plopped off her moccasins and settled into the big arm-chair in front of the easel, curling around this way and that before settling in. The baby-blue angora of her sweater kept dropping off one shoulder—fluffing off as a breeze tosses fuzz from a dandelion to drift here and there.

The first canvas was huge, colors vivid as cartoons. She leaned forward, excited, seeing herself in a new way. Then I showed her another, smaller, a collage: ghostly colors as flowers fade, as red leaves fade, as butterflies fade when pressed into albums.

"Oh," she sighed. "Yes! I see."

"There is one more."

And I showed it to her: a line of yellow encircling the exaggerated roundness of an albino face, the eyes black cherries afloat in a bowl of cream, the mouth a bruised rose petal. She turned away and started to cry.

Just then in walked the kitten. It moved blinking, wavering on the oak floor. With a great sob she ran to kneel beside it: "The dear, the dear . . . the poor dear!"

She lifted it, oh, so gently, and rocked the poor dear, limp as a rag doll, back and forth in her arms, crooning, comforting herself: "It's going to be all right, dear, it's going to be all right."

She kept saying this over and over again.

"Why not call her that? . . . Dear."

"How clever of you, Garnet!"

She held the kitten up and looked at it and with a last quivering sob lay back on the floor nestling Dear between her breasts, quite at peace. I too laid my head back on the chair and closed my eyes, not quite at peace, wondering if and when she and Dear were going to leave. There was something odd about the darkness, as if we were on the edge of passing over a threshold or boundary, and although it was dusk, what light was left had settled into the room with the texture of dawn. Time passed in this confusion, but I couldn't bring myself to move. We never had gotten around to Grafton . . . Still I was exhausted.

A horrendous buzz from the intercom and at the same instant the phone rang. Jane jumped up and ran with Dear to find out who was downstairs, while I picked up the phone. She looked over at me.

"Graf—ton," her lips mimed silently, and without speaking I shook my head back and forth while no no no I screamed inside.

"Claude, may I call you back?" As I said this, on and off,

on and off hard, fast, Jane pressed the door button, saying into the intercom, "Come right up."

"Jane! Why did you do that?" I wanted to kill her.

"I don't *know* why," she said. "I just did."

And there it was, a knocking on the door, knocking knocking, while we stood doing nothing, not even breathing.

" . . . Garnet," he called. "Garnet . . . open up!"

Louder and louder the buzzer kept on and on, and I said, "What the hell, Jane—you let him up, now you let him in."

"My real name's Marygold," she said prissily.

"What the fuck has that to do with it?" I said.

But she just stood there and I couldn't stand it another second so I went and opened the door.

"What are you two doing here in the dark?" he said, and flicked on the light switch just as though he lived here.

"Make yourself at home," I said.

He sprawled on the sofa, stretching his arms, clasping his hands behind his head, leaning back to study the canvases spread around the room.

"My, you've been busy." He smiled.

"Grafton, I hate people dropping in unexpectedly, and I'm late already for a date. Jane is too; she was just leaving."

He glanced at her standing by the door, looking at her for the first time.

"What's *that?*" he said.

"What it appears to be," I said. "A cat, a kitten, a pussy."

"Don't be vulgar," he said.

"Grafton, get out of here!" My voice skidded into a sound I didn't recognize, and I looked behind me to see the stranger who had spoken. Jane shielded Dear's face with her hand as the kitten struggled to escape, claws thrusting into the angora, into Jane.

"Ouch!" she cried. "That hurts."

"You know I don't like cats," he said, "and you know why."

"I don't care what you like or don't like," I said. "I want you out of here."

He gave a colossal sneeze and in the middle of it threw himself at Jane.

She bolted for the door, but he scooped Dear from her by the scruff of the neck, swung her screeching high in the air, back and forth, back and forth . . . Strands of blue angora trailing from her claws, Dear flayed the air as though it were water and she was drowning.

With one hand he opened the window.

Jane, screaming, ran at him, but Dear was already hurtling through the darkness down into the street below.

Jess

AMAGANSETT

A golden afternoon at the beach . . . two children playing on the swing. As the light fades, a voice calls from the house across the way, "Ma-ri-a-aan-na," and the children scatter home like birds flying across the lawn and suddenly the beach is empty.

The day after Katie was born I woke in the hospital flooded with joy—my first thought: I have a baby! And for months after, always the same. Now I wake and my first thought: She's dead.

· · ·

Mine was the first face she saw on this earth and the last.

A sense of doom hangs over everything, as if something terrible is going to happen. But it already has.

There are mornings I can hardly move. I lie on the bed most of the day and cry. Sometimes I think I'm in a dream, one of those dreams that when you wake, the *real* life is the dream and not what you wake to, which is known as the real world. Soon I'll wake and call her up on the phone and say:

"Katie, I had the most terrible dream last night," and I'll start telling her about it, and she'll say:

"Oh, Darling Ma, it was only a dream, everything's all right."

To stay alive I must breathe in and out. I don't have to pretend anymore about anything. I want to die, but no way appeals to me except pills and I reject that because there's always the chance they'll bring me back.

"Moment to moment," Ellie said to me. "God will see you through this. Are you eating?"

I couldn't; I lost ten pounds in three days.

"Eat soft foods," she said. "Rice. Oatmeal. Pureed baby foods. Bananas. Anything you like the taste of. Take care of yourself. Pamper yourself. After Danny died I changed the sheets on my bed every day because it made me feel better. Have a manicure, pedicure, have your hair done. Have a massage. Be good to yourself. Don't do anything you don't want to do. Don't answer letters until you're ready to. There are still some letters about Danny I haven't answered, and it's two years now since he died. Don't go through Katie's things until you're ready to. Don't see anyone you don't want to see. Don't push yourself toward anything you don't want to do. God will get you through this. Call me anytime day or night. I'll be there."

The night it happened, Mac waited at the restaurant. He called the house to find out why I was late. It was after . . . "Do you want me to come?" he said.

But he didn't come.

My intent is not to die, just to disappear—be somewhere else, be someone else . . . someone who is out of pain. It's like when you're visiting somewhere and ready to leave but weary (remembering the long drive back home): if only you could *be* home and not have to *go* home.

Skinned alive . . . But I don't die. I must be alive, because I have lived through another minute, and now I know there is the rest of my life to get through.

Katie and I on the veranda, sitting in the swing. It's hot and we swing back and forth back and forth having a long discussion about popcorn at the movies. Should we go to see *Psycho II* just to be able to get movie popcorn? Instead, we go to the A & P and buy it there to pop at home; Pepperidge Farm Cappucino cookies, Good Humors, Popsicles and chocolate-covered peanuts too, for later. Giggles in the supermarket, dropping our purchases into the cart. Driving home to the music on the car radio, an old recording of Ray Noble singing "After you, who? could supply my sky of blue— After you, who? could I love."

Something intervened, and there was an accident. I was there when it happened. Now everything is changed. Even Dolores is perceived in a new way. I don't know why.

Constantly I replay the scene: There is something I could have done to stop it from happening—had I been there minutes earlier—had she heard me when I shouted, Go back! Go back! If I'd run faster, gotten to her as she reached out to me, pulled her away before the car hit—thrown myself in front of it—it wouldn't have happened. Over and over in my mind I replay it. Sometimes in slow motion, other times fast—in reverse. But it was like being on a roller coaster—when it was happening nothing could have stopped it.

Something intervened. An accident. A shipwreck. There was a raft, and I climbed on. Later I came to know it was my bed. Other survivors climbed on with me; some drowned, some became deranged. Some were strong. Katie's friends gave strength so that I could give it back to them. As I lay there and they sat beside me on the raft or stood talking low across the room I could transmit myself into their skin. Sylvie looks like me, could be my daughter, and Linda has my eyes and mouth, resembles me even more. Later, outside, I could transmit myself

into people walking or seen from a taxi window—strangers.
And animals—a dog walking in the park—I became.

Mac kept calling and calling, although he had been told not
to. "Do you want me to come?" he'd said. That he had to *ask*
. . . My dear love is someone I don't know at all.

When I went out on the street for the first time, everything
was as usual—people and crowds and traffic and taxis and coming and going, just as if nothing had happened. I walked on a
tree-lined street on the West Side, slowly. The sun shimmered
through the branches, making shadows tremble on the pavement. I walked into them and stopped. On the top floor of a
house, a window was open: someone was playing the piano in
an upstairs room. I looked up at the window, listening. A gate
in front of the house had been left open—open for me. I knew
that if I could walk through the gate, on through the door,
into the house and up the stairs to the top room, I would become
someone else, someone out of pain.

Walking again on the same street, I looked down, and centered
neatly on the pavement at my feet—a postcard, a postcard from
far away. The lettering on it was somehow familiar . . . block
lettering, like the lettering I had used long ago at Aunt Frayne's
in Santa Barbara. The message facing up was a message for
someone else but also a message for me . . . an answer perhaps
to those notes I had passed through the narrow necks of bottles
and sent across the sea:

Dearest Oscar:

    Hope all is well with you and yours – I am back in Holland & I must say it is a pleasure! The weather is not at all like NY – rainy & cold in the 50's – what a change from the blistering heat – My Mom sends her regards & many well wishes for your Mom also of course –

Take good care –

Marianne

Destiny. Some choices and decisions can be made, but the large pattern is preset. From the moment we are born—for you, for me, for Katie—the plan is already set, with logic and order behind it. It's just not understood yet.

Ken has been taking care of business for me until things change. One night he came by to help me with letters. I lay on the raft breathing in and out while he sat cross-legged on the floor in front of the fire, opening envelopes. The ones I want to respond to are put in one basket and into another go the letters requiring only card acknowledgments. None from Garnet. I hadn't thought of it until now but how strange I haven't heard from her—I hope she's all right. Letters come even from people I don't know. Strangers who have heard about Katie, strangers who have lost a child. We are not alone.

"Hang on, Mrs. Weatherbee."

    Jim Dayton, a classmate of Katie's, said this to me at a

moment when I thought I wasn't going to make it. I keep
hearing him say this when I am alone.

Mac finally stopped calling.

I reside below sea level.

I descend to another level of grief, taking a moment to become
accustomed—a deep breath through the nose, out through the
mouth . . . After a time comes the balance I need to survive
in this alien territory. (Yet I feel closer to myself than I ever
have.)

Katie,
     I don't know how to start this. It's a letter to you but
really a letter to myself.
     I believe there is logic in the world that comes from the
great intelligence we call God and that there is a reason
therefore for all things and that we have been placed here
with a logic we do not understand yet. The pain I knew
when I lost my mother Dolores I used to think was my
test and that nothing could ever hurt me in that way again.
It lay there inside me just under my breasts, a hard diamond, a center no one could reach or take from me. But
it's gone now and I'm immersed in another place, a place
I can never leave. Walking on the beach would always

ground me—that unrelenting leveler the sea. But now I am *in* that sea, not walking beside it, descended to a place I didn't know existed, rock bottom, from which there is no escape or deeper place to go, or place to hide.

Love,

Mom

P.S. I may be wrong. Perhaps what appears to be rock bottom is a trick and soon I will descend to a deeper level.

Another day has gone by, Katie. I miss you. Sometimes I feel you close to me. Then there are times when you are lost to me, and only pain is there and I know it will never go away.

Katie, are you all right? Are you with Daddy? Are you close to him as you are to me? Is it going to be all right, or should I get through the door to you now?

Sometimes I think it's all a joke and that you're coming back.

Katie—hi
It's your "Darling Ma"
I love you Katie
Please don't leave me

Katie: A dream. In the distance you and I are walking (on a beach) at the edge of the sea, we are walking away side by side—two figures, you in your black coat, I also in black, my hair hanging down my back—side by side we walk away together but not touching.

Katie, sometimes when my eyes are closed you come to me as a ball of light, aqua blue brilliant as the sun, closer, closer, until you surround me. Then a long time can go by and I am out of touch. When you come back I know that death is but the leaving of one dimension for another and that it exists on this planet and those who die have broken through into light and although we cannot see our dead they surround us.

P.P.S. There is a place where you wait for me, I know, and so there is no Good-bye for us. Things will happen as they are meant to happen. With the same logic that took you from me. I'll write more later.

Katie, what was it you were so anxious to tell me? So important that you ran against the light.

Garnet

NEW YORK CITY

Production on the series has to stop until Jane recovers. After the police came and took Grafton away she stayed here and next day they brought her things over from the Wyndham. At first the doctors thought she'd have to go into the hospital, but when they said Payne Whitney I said no, I'd take care of her, be responsible for her. She relies on me for everything, and I enjoy this, although she can be pretty infantile and impossible at times, needing endless reassurances about her looks, her weight, even her talent, for which I used to think she had a hefty esteem. I haven't gotten any work done since it happened. How typical of Grafton to think he could get away with it, do that and then have everything be the same as it was. But it's brought Janey and me close together. That's the only good thing that can be said about any of it.

"I feel better," she said. She was touching up the roots of her hair with peroxide, engrossed by the details in the bathroom mirror.

"You look it," I said.

"Let's send out for Chinese food."

"Why not go out somewhere?"

"Umm . . ." she said, moving her granny glasses down on the bridge of her nose and leaning over the basin to get closer to the mirror. "Better wait till I go on the set. Someone might see me."

"When do you think you'll go back?"

She'd become enraptured by an angle of her face newly discovered and said absently, "Tomorrow or the day after."

In a way I was sorry. I'd become quite attached to the mood of my studio, which had taken on the camaraderie of a college dorm—midnight snacks and rap sessions.

"I'm going to miss you, Jelly-Jane."

"Well, I could stay." She looked at me from the mirror. "A while longer . . . What do you think?"

"I don't think I'd get much work done, that's what I think."

"Oh, Garnet—I'd be out so early, back late and . . . it might be nice."

She dabbed some Laszlo pHelityl cream under her eyes and put an extra dab on the tip of her nose, quite enchanted.

"You know, Garnet . . . I almost wish you hadn't called the coppers that night—"

"Jane! Come on."

"This is the best bathroom light I've ever seen," she said, switching it off. She went over to her purse on the bed and took out a big heart-shaped lollipop in pink cellophane.

"Well . . ." Lolling back on the bed and crinkling off the wrapper. "He *is* allergic to cats and he just took it the wrong way—it was my fault, really, for getting Dear in the first place."

She licked the lollipop and after a while perched the granny glasses on the top of her head. Soon there would be nothing but the stick and she querulously examined the bit of candy that was left.

"I hope he gets a judge whose wife is on the board." I was quite fed up with her.

"Board of what?" she said, turning over on her stomach and pressing her face into the pillow.

"The board of the ASPCA, that's what!" I said.

Quite suddenly she started to sob. I moved quickly, sitting beside her on the bed to comfort her, but as I did she turned over, and she was laughing, hysterically.

"If only he could have seen his face when you actually did it—and then when they arrived—he couldn't believe it!"

"And now you wish . . ."

"Well—I don't. Still . . ."

"Still *what*?" I said.

She closed her eyes and gave a sigh, quite convincing.

"Well," I said, "he's finished for me. Anyway, even when I

was most attracted to him there were great hunks of time when I didn't even think about him."

"Oh, I always did. Even when I wasn't thinking about him, I was."

"That's what I mean."

She sat up and put her arms around me. "You're much more fun to be with than he is and I'm afraid of him now so please let me stay."

"Well—I don't know if it's such a good idea."

"You know how you love to paint me. I'll be your model."

"I'd like that."

"And I'm really all right now. All those silly notions, running naked into the street and all that—just spur-of-the-moment impulses. I don't have bad dreams anymore either, at least not many, or even think much about . . . Dear."

But now she really did start to cry and I told her to stay as long as she liked, until she felt stronger and more herself. And that's how I got myself into it.

Jane

If only Garnet were a man . . . Right now everything's super, but how long can it last? When the telly series is over, what then, pray?

"Garnet, if only you were a man."

"But I'm not," she said.

I wonder if he's all right.

"Garnet, don't you think it strange we haven't heard from Grafton?"

"It shows a decency in him I hadn't expected," she said, cold as ice.

"Not that it matters one way or another—it just seems odd."

"Maybe the ASPCA's put him to sleep."

"Oh, Garnet—how unlike you to say such a cruel thing," I said sweetly.

"I thought you never wanted to see him again."

So we were back to that again.

"I don't!" I told her. And it's true. I don't. Still . . .

Jess

Back in New York the days slip by, weeks. Soon it will be years. It's then I'll see him. Mac. Quite by chance. But I won't recognize him. The person coming toward me is one of the many strangers I pass in the crowded street.

There are days possessed by loss and the want of him and it comes to me that the want of him is as the want of another . . . Dolores.

The Diaries of Dolores Willis

THE GORKY SANITARIUM

Brillianta is forsaking me. No, they are not taking her away, *she* is leaving, for they now agree she is "capable of taking care of herself." Capable! If only they knew! However, I am consoled by the fact that she'll be back in no time flat, once those doctors see how she does when she tries ice skating on her own, without me to hold her up. So let her go, the faithless one, this is not Good-bye. All I have to do is wait.

My mistake was when I started comprehending the things Nico spoke of instead of letting them pass through me. But I wanted to be close, as close as could be to him, and this is what made me make such an effort to understand. In the beginning it was only his beloved voice I heard; the words had little meaning as I memorized, repeated them to myself. Then in time even my speech patterns became his, became knowledgeable as though I understood. It was in this way I became aware that Nico was part of a plan, far-reaching, of world-shaking importance—the biggest event in Russian history. At first it had little reality to me; only later, when I visualized the terrors, what was being done to those who were innocent, to animals, to lovers who loved as Nico and I, did doubt begin to poison me, take possession of my being, obsess my every breath and finally seep into my love, my great love for Nicolai.

Brillianta Vosvi

MOSCOW

Farewells have been exchanged with all those left behind in the hated Gorky. The only one I was sorry to say Good-bye to was Dolores and so, already starting to miss her, I took it upon myself to borrow one or two of her Diaries, knowing where she hides them, and now they are well preserved in my care to peruse whenever I get lonely for her.

They are most interesting these Diaries of Dolores and the more I read them the more interesting they become. Now more than ever do I believe her to be a well-connected personage in the United States of America. But why was this American lady amongst us and why does she remain in the hated Gorky? In these pages may be the answer. It is what I intend to know and I will succeed, for persistence is one of my finest attributes. I hope when she notices some of her Diaries are missing it doesn't send her into one of her states or worse still make her attack the nurses for stealing them. I would have had the courtesy to ask her for them before I left but knowing she would refuse, I resorted to questionable means. There was no other recourse.

The love between Dolores and Nicolai Voznesensky is most interesting to me of all the interesting things Dolores writes in her Diaries. How fed up he must have been at times with her childish concern about the killing of animals in his five-year plan. Could it be that she is not cognizant of his former importance? Certainly she is unaware that he is dead, which, of course, I know, thanks to my brother Miron Semenovich—tried and executed without publicity, certainly the wisest method in such a situation. As I recall, it was just before the canary was inserted into my head by that dwarfish heavy-jawed uncouth dummkopf. Dear Madre Dolores, how she looked forward, counting on the happy day when her Nico would appear and take her away, out of the hated Gorky . . . No chance, of course, just a simpleminded hope she could cling to.

It is a different matter now that I have been released. I am a serious person, not one of those flibbertigibbets. Also I am discreet and discreet people attract other discreet people and it is through this that tomorrow I have an appointment at the American Embassy where it is my intention to place the Diaries of Dolores in the proper hands. They'll sit up and take notice or I'll eat my chapeau—as Madre would say.

Jess

NEW YORK CITY

A call today from Washington. The FBI asking if I will receive a visit regarding a private matter. The tone implied discretion, further conversation discouraged. What can it be?

Dolores may be alive. There's a woman in a sanitarium in Russia who's been there since 1933, a woman who may be my mother.

And if it is Dolores? Since Katie died, although Dolores's photographs surround me as they always have, they are unfamiliar to me, images of a woman I don't know.

THE CURTAIN RISES

A long corridor of the Ritz Hotel in Paris, where a tall, thin, very beautiful lady in a long yellow velvet dress and ropes of pearls is seen. She moves down the corridor away from us, about to disappear around a corner.

JESSICA, *calling out:* Mummy . . . Mummy . . .

LADY *turns and stands looking at Jessica running toward her:* Why, Jessica . . . It is you, isn't it? . . . What are you doing here?

JESSICA, *crying and trying to climb the ropes of pearls to reach her:* Mummy . . . Mummy . . . I never thought I'd find you.

LADY: My! you haven't grown at all . . .

The ropes of pearls break as Jessica keeps trying to climb up to reach the lady, whose hands are just out of reach. The beads scatter on the floor.

JESSICA: Oh, Mummy . . . Mummy—I broke your necklace!

LADY: It doesn't matter, darling—nothing matters now we've found each other . . .

JESSICA, *slipping and skidding around on the beads, still reaching up to the lady:* Why did you leave me . . . why? Why, Mummy? Why?

LADY: I didn't—I didn't. Someone—now who was it?—someone took me dancing and I just never came back.

JESSICA: I thought it was my fault . . .

LADY: Why, child, you've done nothing but break my necklace and scatter my pearls hither and yon . . . Pick them up for me, will you, darling—they'll easily be restrung . . .

THE CURTAIN FALLS

The Diaries of Dolores Willis

THE GORKY SANITARIUM

No longer am I the inexperienced woman of the world that I was when I first found myself in this monastic hellhole—no longer the innocent left to the whims of those who come and go through these halls of white shadows. I know what I know and I know Brillianta has left, said a tearful Good-bye to me, and as I think back on this sobbing farewell, I see in hindsight— ah yes, that great illuminator—that something else lurked behind her simpering bye-bye, for her eyes shifted away from my glance, shot away, in fact, as I tried to anchor them to mine, and now I know *why*. Naughty naughty girl. Hateful vile girl. Naughty naughty Marietta. Not brilliant Brillianta. Sneaky Brillianta, with undesirable ways of doing things, things like stealing—for that's what she's done: *stolen* my Diaries. Not even the courtesy to make a clean sweep did she have—only one or two, here and there, she took, thinking by this childish ruse to trick me so I would not notice the infamy she had perpetrated. And those pathetic tears as she tore herself from my arms I now know to have been but chips of ice falling falling down onto my shoulder, melting as they touched the warmth of my tender skin. That in itself should have warned me. Ah! perfidious one. But I shall forgive you. Or maybe I won't. On the one hand I may be so *enchantée* to see your stupid face again that I'll let it pass without comment; on the other hand I may decide to slap your pretty hand, for you are not the hand that feeds, or the foot either, for that matter. Plenty of nurses around here to do that—remember? Come to think of it, a good grind on your foot with my heel may be the best solution. *Tempus fugit*—only time will tell.

Jess

NEW YORK CITY

As I lay in my bed last night Abe took possession of my body, he took my soul into his arms, and struggling up from sleep in fierce surrender I was afraid, for his arms clung to me like steel in the dark. Then, as he entered me, he called my name, assuring me that it was he and not a stranger, and as I came to know that this was true, I cried out in joy, for the pain of missing him was gone and all was as it had been when we were lovers long ago in splendor. But when I called his name no sound was heard, for his lips were on mine and the wild beauty drove us into battle, fighting to hold on each to the other, for time was short—he had come from elsewhere and must return, to that place I could not follow . . . As he slipped away, more desperate we became, but I was pulled back into the place I knew so well before this joy had come to be.

Still, he was here, I know. And it is strange to think upon.

.   .   .

When I go to the graves I stand numb, staring down at the names cut into the flat gray stones. The grass between them grows smooth and green as it waits for me.

Katie and I went to Paris the year after Abe died. We stayed at the Hôtel de Nice on the rue des Beaux Arts. Our last morning, waking at six, I looked out from the balcony into the silent courtyard below, thinking about Dolores and my father, who had come here on their honeymoon, stayed perhaps in this very room. Breakfast—the chicory *café au lait*, scalloped butter pats—*en retard* that day, the croissants not ready from the oven at such an early hour. Katie was asleep as I efficiently rustled around, attending to the last-minute details of departure. As *café complet* arrived, she sat up sleepily.

"What time are we leaving, Ma?"

"Soon . . ."

"Yes, Big Chief," she said, jumping out of bed.

Abe's last words to me:

"This is a terrible thing to do to you and Katie."

Garnet

Sometimes I'll leave the radio by my bed on, to let myself drift through the night in and out of music in and out of myself as I drift in and out of sleep . . . Toward dawn the "Habanera" of Chabrier and with it . . . a shadow coming toward me—but from where?—calling out to me . . . Katie Weatherbee? Yes, of course. Not a shadow at all but the way she was, running up the stairs that afternoon calling to Jess: "Darling Ma . . ." Then, as she comes closer, the music pulls me back, into itself, and I give myself to it, falling falling into a dream about having a child, a child who turns out to be Katie, but when I look upon her for the first time it isn't Katie. It's me.

Jess

Ken came again to help me with the letters. He took one at random from the pile, opened it . . .

"Jess . . . it's from Mac."

A hand-delivered letter. No date, only my name and *Personal* written lower left on the envelope.

Dear Jessa,

What can I say what can anyone say my heart goes out to you my love. I know you will come out of the forest and see the green hills. I know knowing you that life will be wonderful again. You have a lot to give. Remember please I want to help. As all your many friends want to help.

I love you
Mac

He's in Angola. Ken found out for me. So there's no way of reaching him. All I can do is wait . . .

Garnet

I just learned about it, quite by accident. Two women were talking, sitting next to me at the counter having coffee. Katie's dead. I can't believe it. While I was in Paris with Claude. That's when it happened. What a tragedy, one woman said, and then the other asked if Baryshnikov had a new girlfriend and they started talking about Jessica Lange and Sam Shepard and I went to the phone hanging on the wall by the pastries and called Jess.

Jess

It is spring and the fireplace in the library has been filled with acanthus leaves to replace the logs of winter. Garnet and I sit facing each other as we did that autumn evening long ago— and I expect to see Katie coming through the door, but the moment passes and I know she won't because she is dead.

Garnet reaches out her hand to me. "Are you all right?"

"I'm doing O.K.," I tell her. It is important to me to sound sane, normal.

I start to say something about Katie but instead find myself saying, "There's a woman in a sanitarium in Russia believed to be Dolores—"

"Oh, Jess, how amazing that would be!"

"I'm not sure anymore . . . Even if it is my mother, we may not recognize each other."

"Oh, you will—how can you doubt it?"

"My memory of her is the way *you* are, Garnet—your hair, your eyes, the way you move. Why, she even wore a necklace of red beads with a red dress, just as you are now. She was twenty-seven when she disappeared—more than fifty years ago . . . I don't even know now—strange as it must sound—if I want to see her."

"It's not strange at all, Jess . . . How can you have any reality right now except Katie?"

She unclasps her necklace and hands it to me. "Here—take them; they have a warmth few stones have."

"They're garnets, aren't they?" I hold them up to the light.

"Jess . . . they're yours for as long as you want."

The beads are irregular in shape, with a mysterious darkness, yet how warm they are, satiny—not like stones at all but pebbles smoothed by the night-dark sea and left by a wave on the sand, magnets to draw in the hot day sun. I clasp them around my neck and start to cry.

"They'll bring strength, Jess—you'll see . . ."

"Maybe she won't know me and I'll be lost to her, but not in the way that Katie is lost to me—do you understand?"

"Yes—I do, I think."

"Since it happened . . . I feel connected to everyone in the world in a way I never did before, but if Dolores denies me—it will be as though a link in the chain has been broken."

"It doesn't have to be that way," Garnet says.

How lightly the beads rest upon my skin. I lean back, closing my eyes—so tired as Garnet's voice filters through to me, low and gentle like Dolores's, soft as the rain gently falling on a roof of leaves.

" . . . Grafton . . ."

"Grafton?"

I was wide awake.

"He's the man I lived with on and off—that is, when he was in New York."

"Grafton Davis?" I asked.

"Why, yes. Do *you* know him?"

"And when he was in London he lived with someone else," I said.

"How did you know that?"

She was quite startled.

"And you're in love with him," I went on.

She got up and went over to the mantel and bent down to brush her hands over the acanthus leaves.

"It's such a pretty thing to do"—she traced her finger along a shiny leaf—"leaves in the fireplace for spring in place of logs."

"Dolores always did that in the house in Paris for the summer. Even when we left for Cannes or Deauville and the dust sheets went on the furniture and there was no one there to enjoy them."

"It's complicated," she said. "Grafton. I guess you could say I was . . . in love with him once, but it all depends on how you define love."

"How do *you?*" I said.

"I don't. It was like drinking salt water and always being thirsty."

"He *is* attractive," I said.

"And were *you* in love with him?"

"I saw quite a lot of him after Abe died—it's a fuzzy time in my mind. I was numb and Grafton happened to wander by. I did things I would never have done if—"

"So he *did* talk to you about me."

She was guarded, uncertain.

"Only that there was someone here in New York he lived with and another someone in London he lived with when he was there."

"Jane." Garnet nodded.

"Yes—Jane Esmond." I smiled.

"So you knew *her* name," Garnet said, "but not mine?"

"Oh, he never told me," I said quickly. "He's much too secretive for that. I found out quite by chance . . . How I agonized over you both, knowing you had a permanence in his life I'd never have."

"Jess, he's not worth it—"

"Oh, but that has nothing to do with it—"

"Yes, he has that effect on people."

"Do you know Jane Esmond?" I asked her.

She hesitated and fished around in her purse until she found a cigarette.

"I didn't know you smoked," I said.

"Actually, Jane's here in New York . . . staying with me."

She lit the cigarette and breathed deeply.

"And where's Grafton?"

"In a lot of trouble." She snuffed out the cigarette.

"Trouble? What kind of trouble?"

"It's a long story," she said wearily.

"What's she like?"

"Not at all what you might imagine. She's such a good actress you'd think she'd be so sure of herself, but she's the most unsure-of-herself person I've ever known—frets constantly about her looks, her body and its maintenance, though she has no cause to, for she's exercised all her life and kept herself lovely as she could wish."

"Does he still say 'Ditto'?"

We both smiled.

"When you say 'I love you'—oh yes!"

"And he still takes his orange juice squeezer with him no matter where he hangs his hat?"

"Ah yes, fresh orange juice a necessity for breakfast no matter what!"

"I never thought you and I would be sitting here talking like this about him. I haven't really given him a thought in years."

And I hadn't. He was a stranger to me and . . . *that* Jess was too, someone I didn't even know. Only once in a while, maybe when the black cashmere scarf came to hand, the very thing for a chilly day, I'd think of him . . .

"Come to think of it," I said to Garnet, "I still have a scarf he gave me . . ."

She smiled. "Oh yes—he's big on scarves."

We both laughed.

"But he never went too far, at least not with me. He always knew when to stop."

"Yes, he has that knack," Garnet said.

"So he's in trouble?"

"Not that kind of trouble. The ASPCA is after him for throwing Jane's kitten out the window."

"But that's awful!"

"Jane almost had a breakdown over it—that's why she's staying with me instead of at the Wyndham."

"What's going to happen?"

"We don't know yet. Jane's frightened of him but she still wants him back."

"Oh, Garnet—how I tormented myself over you and that

Jane—and here we are friends, much closer than Grafton and I ever were."

"Ditto for me and Janey. You'd like her, Jess. That is, if she could ever be straight with you. She's always playacting—doesn't trust herself to be herself because she doesn't know who she really is."

And there we sat, two friends, gossiping on an afternoon in spring. A west wind was blowing and with it perhaps would be a peace, a settling down, for it's not tempestuous, this wind, but gentle and seductive, it lulls while it quickens the listening spirit . . . Springtime, with summer coming along soon, maybe even tomorrow, and for a moment I can breathe again, as if Katie weren't dead, as if Dolores would be coming home any minute now and everything were all right.

Garnet

I'd decided not to tell Janey about Jess and Grafton—after all, it had nothing to do with the goings-on now. But when I got back, of course out it popped. It fell rather flat, though, preoccupied as she was with other things—mainly her toes, for she was giving herself a pedicure.

"Well—he called," she said finally.

"And you hung up on him."

" . . . Not exactly."

"You're not going to see him?"

"Garnet! I'm surprised at you. No! I'm not going to see him, but he's very contrite—in his way."

"Yes—I know all about his way."

"Honestly, Garnet, I feel a bit sorry for him. He's genuinely worried about what the ASPCA's going to do—"

"I bet he is!"

"And very vexed over the publicity, only because it was Jane Esmond's cat, he says—pushed him unfairly into the limelight, et cetera et cetera et cetera—"

"So now it's *your* fault?"

"I didn't say that—"

"You did a few days ago."

"Only because I was in a blue mood."

"And what color is your mood now, pray tell?"

"Pink—pearly peachy pink," she said, holding up the bottle of nail polish and shaking it up and down.

"Janey—don't you see what he's doing?"

She started scanning a big magnifying glass over her toes and testing each one to see if the polish was dry.

"Pretty, isn't it? The latest thing—Mermaid Coral."

"So how did it end?"

"What?"

"The conversation."

"Oh—you know—he really misses us."

"I bet!"

"Garnet—what was I supposed to do—bang the phone down?"

She hobbled peevishly across to the closet, all the while endeavoring to keep her toes apart, and she pulled out one of her Sadie Thompson dresses.

"Oh well—I might as well tell you: he's picking me up—"

"Not *here* he's not!"

"Oh, Garnet, simmer down. I told him you were indisposed and that I'd meet him downstairs at eight."

"Really, Jane—how can you, after—"

"Don't be a pill." She pouted, holding up the dress and waddling over to the full-length mirror. "He's never seen me in this one before and you know how he likes me in charmeuse. What do you think?"

Of course I didn't answer, but even if I had she wouldn't have heard, lost as she was in her reflection, quite desperately seeking someone, someone she could recognize.

"Oh, darling," I said.

But I'd been right—she didn't hear me.

Jess

This was the message:

"Jessa—it's Mac, calling from London. I just got off the plane. I must talk to you, please please—this is the last call I'll make to you but please please, Jessa, call me—I'm at the Westbury 011-44-1-629-7755, Room 105—please please, Jessa . . ."

"I didn't think I'd ever hear your voice again—the night it happened—I tried to get to you that night but—"

"When you didn't come—"

"I did, I did, but I couldn't get through—you don't know what it was like—the police, crowds—"

"I know that now, knew it as soon as I read your letter—"

The words kept tumbling together.

"I love your nose," he said. "You have a beautiful nose—

have you noticed when I kiss you I always kiss your nose as well—"

"Oh God," I moaned. "I can't believe we're talking—"

"After it happened—when I went to Angola—all I could eat were bananas—I thought I'd never see you again—"

"Me too," I said. "All I could eat were bananas—"

"Oh God, Jessa—thinking I'd never see you again made me know how much I loved you, and I felt so terrible knowing you'd never know it or that I had come to you that night, had tried every day after to see you but you wouldn't—"

"You were dead to me."

"And when I did get you on the phone you hung up on me, wouldn't listen, and I couldn't get through, no one would let me."

"I told everyone not to, and then I changed the number—all except the office—and still you kept calling—oh, darling."

"I imagined I'd run into you years later—Cap Ferrat or somewhere—and that you'd say hello to me as you would to a stranger."

"Not even that—I would have cut you dead."

"I'll be back the day after tomorrow."

All has shifted, adjusted, changed and is changing. There is nothing for me to do. That Mac is married is now of no importance.

An accident was about to happen.

But it didn't.

This is how it was
But as I think this
I know
It did
Happen.

Mac takes me for promenades in the park. Today we sat on a bench watching children sail toy boats on the pond.

"I desire you in every way," he said.

Garnet

I stand behind the door, a Victorian caricature with a rolling pin, waiting for hubby to come home, only instead of a hubby it's a Janey. Suddenly I find myself in a tug-of-war with Grafton for her soul and I'm damned if I know why.

She called at midnight from somewhere. "What are you doing?" she said, easy as you please.

"What are *you* up to is more like it," I said.

She giggled, and in the background, laughter—Grafton.

"Grafton says to say hi."

"Tell him I'm not interested."

"Garnet says she's not interested."

More giggling and then, "Hey, Pussycat, why don't you come on over?"

"Put Jane back on," I said. But he wouldn't and so I hung up on him and now I'm more miserable than ever. Is she all right?

She came in at noon the next day, more or less intact considering she hadn't slept.

"Where were you?" I asked.

"I'll tell you later," she said, and she collapsed on the sofa in her Bo-Peep dress, which was all wrinkled anyway, and fell asleep. She had a bruise on her arm. A quite nasty one. The only one, or were there others?

"Oh, Garnet—don't nag at me." She'd just gotten out of her bath and was patting herself dry and twisting around trying to examine the bruise on her bottom. "He never touches my face," she said, quite pleased with herself.

"Here," I said, giving her a hand mirror. "This'll make it easier."

"How thoughtful," she said cattily.

"Why did you even bother to come back?" I asked.

"But, Garnet—" She was surprised.

"Why didn't you stay with him?"

"I didn't know you cared," she said coyly.

"Well, I do. How can you think so little of yourself to spend even a minute of time with him?"

"He makes me feel alive—"

"And what do I make you feel?"

"Myself." She reached her hand out to me and I took it.

"Janey, look at me," I said.

But she pulled away and, still holding the mirror, went over to the window and stood naked, looking out into the street.

"Why do you put yourself down?" I said.

She kept looking out into the street and after a while said to no one in particular, "I don't when I'm acting."

"But you're always acting—off stage as well as on."

She turned around and put her arms over her breasts. "So is everybody else—only I do it better because I'm a pro!"

She was cold, and I went into the bathroom and got a terry towel and put it around her.

"How can you trust anyone if you really believe that?" I said.

"Trust? Oh, I don't." She lifted her head proudly.

"That's the saddest thing you could say—"

"But how can I trust if no one including myself *is* real?"

"And what about me?"

"You, Garnet . . ." She held up the hand mirror and gazed into it. "Mirror mirror on the wall, who is fairest of them all?" she chanted, and held it out at arm's length for me to look into, saying grandly: "Garnet is real and therefore fairest of them all."

But am I? Real. Isn't she perhaps right? Don't we all invent each other in countless ways we are unaware of and pretend for reasons best unknown to ourselves? I thought of my father and how little he comes to mind and yet how constantly I think of him and Pepper Pearl, and now that I was thinking of him I also thought of Grafton, and then my mind skidded on to something else (perhaps Jess?), but what it was kept eluding me and so I said to Janey, "If you'd only stop the make-believe for five minutes you might find you actually enjoyed being yourself."

"Maybe, but it's too risky." She went and lay down on the bed, with the towel over her face. "Anyway, what I'm dying for right now is one of those Arden treatments—a silent attendant in a pink smock brushing my body with hot paraffin, all pink, and then wrapping me in wax paper, and I'll lie in a dark room until the pink wax cools and makes a shell around my pink body, and after eternity the silent attendant will return to unveil me, peel off the pink wax, anoint my body with unguents and sweet oils before massage."

"What about those bruises?"

"Oh, I'd think of something: a fall from a horse or—not that it's any of the silent pink-smocked attendant's business."

So I said, "I see—pain, then pleasure."

But she wasn't listening.

Jess

Although it has been months—it happened yesterday. Katie . . .

There is no word from Moscow, and Dolores has drifted into landscape. Mac showed me a picture today of his mother. It's reminiscent of a 1912 photograph I've seen of Maude Adams in a Barrie play, delicate, with the sense of a secret withheld. After this I was able to look at the photographs of Dolores and see her more clearly. Still it is as if I hold opera glasses, unable to get the image quite in focus. When I do, I'll be ready to meet her—when the time comes, if it does.

"You dwell out of time," Mac says, closing his eyes.

We are cozily stretched out at opposite ends of the sofa. I've taken off his socks and am giving him a foot rub.

"Like in a movie . . ." He is musing. "At the end there's an old man and he sees coming toward him, down the garden path, the girl he loved, as she was—young. Nothing has changed although he's old."

I love that idea. It reminds me of me and my mother. But I don't say so.

"I feel we've always been together; I'm vulnerable in a way I've never been before. I want us to be in London together, I want you to go everywhere with me—I want us to have a history."

We sit close, close on a bench in the park. A woman with a huge red-and-green parrot on her shoulder walks by.

"What's his name?" Mac calls out.

"Jericho." She waves and walks on out of sight.

He touches the brim of my hat and says, "Kiss me, look at me. I'll never fail you."

The way he came inside me yesterday afternoon so gently at first and after asking if it gave me any pleasure that way. Yes! for it implies a greater intimacy.

After he left he called from the phone booth at the corner.

"I hate to say Good-bye to you. I don't know how to say Good-bye."

Billie

Last night I caught Maclin heading out the door with Boon on a leash.

"It's raining," I said.

He didn't bother to answer.

He hardly ever walks Boon—he puts him on the terrace—
and it made me fume, this sudden outing in the rain with that
dog, so I put on my sou'wester and shadowed them along the
street. It wasn't far, because what he wanted came along soon
enough—the phone booth two blocks away. In he went and
stood there talking for eight minutes—I timed it—with Boon
shuffling about in the downpour, nagging at his leash. Who's
he after this time?

It's that Jessica Weatherbee! I followed him again and saw them
together in the park, walking and then for a long time sitting
on a bench, talking. He sat close to her and kept touching her
hair, kissing her, not rough at all, gently like he meant it, and
looking at her, really looking. She wore a panama hat that
shaded her face from the sun. It had a black ribbon around the
brim. She's thin, much thinner than I am. And taller. I hate
her.

Her kid was killed in an automobile accident. She was that
dancer Katerina Willis—twenty, Jenny's age. Now he'll never
leave her.

Jess

MOSCOW

This city is as unfamiliar to me as the secret places in my mind
where my mother lives, for although I have prepared myself,

now that I am here another reality has taken hold. The woman in the sanitarium is Dolores and I have come to Moscow to bring her home. How do you say Hello to someone you've never said Good-bye to?

She has been moved from the Gorky Sanitarium to Spaso House, the official residence of the U.S. ambassador. I have been warned that she is fragile. Have they warned her that I too am fragile? But how could they know this, when I hide it even from myself?

Down endless corridors up an endless staircase along another endless corridor until at last a door opens and I enter a large room with sunlight zigzagging against walls lacquered the yellow of a Chinese ceremonial robe. Far away in this room of yellow a tall thin woman sits straight in a golden chair, idly fanning herself with a yellow rice-paper fan, and although the gauzy robe she wears is white, there is reflected in its folds the yellow hues of the sunlight. For a dazed moment she is the Pre-Raphaelite princess in the wheelchair. But I close my eyes against this, dismiss it as a trick—reshuffling, allowing the image to sift away so that I can return to the safety of memory, to the way she was—my mother, Dolores. I walk toward her slowly so as not to startle her, but she does not see me as I approach and for a moment I think that she is blind.

"Mummy?"

She turns toward me and I know that she is not blind, she is frightened, more frightened than I am. I sit on the stool beside her chair and take her hand, but she pulls away and I say, "Mummy—it's Jessica."

She looks past me to the door at the far end of the room, but when it remains closed, she loses interest and looks to me. "Who are you?" she says.

"Jessica," I say and again take her hand, but she is angry now.

"I had a little daughter once—Jessica—but I'm sane enough to know it's not *you*."

The sunlight shifts, hits her face, and she opens the rice-paper fan to shield herself against the brightness. Her hair is long, as I remember it, but white, so white, pale as bleached sea grasses, and her eyes, pale aquamarine, look through me toward the door, waiting . . .

"When is she coming?" she asks.

Her skin too has faded, blurring the nose into a rounded softness, and her mouth, once so red against the pale skin, now disappears into the planes of her face. The long red-lacquered fingernails she so prided herself on are now short and hastily filed, untended.

"Do you remember the yellow velvet dress and your long ropes of pearls?"

"How would you know about that—or the pearls?"

"I remember you in that dress—and the pearls. I've been keeping them for you."

"How kind of you," she said. "But why?"

"Because I'm Jessica—your daughter."

"Nico likes that dress." She smiled. "The color of sun, he says, and my hair black velvet—the mystery of night."

In the dark I cry out for you Mother Mother Mother. I have never stopped searching for you, in every face I saw, around every corner, in every person I loved.

But she doesn't hear me. How could she, for I say these things in silence.

"Whose child are you if not mine?" she asked.

"Don't think about that now," I said. "Don't think about anything except yourself and feeling strong again."

"I am tired." She reached over to the table beside her chair and pressed a bell. "What did you say your name was? I don't remember seeing you before—you must be new here. Maybe you would be so kind as to help me find out what's happened to Brillianta Vosvi—she's left me and I'm very put out with her, very!"

The door opened and she stood up. "Oh, it's only you," she said to the nurse, and together we guided Dolores back to the curtained darkness of her chamber, where she lay down on the bed. I covered her and started to leave, but as I did she reached her hand out to me and said: "Stay."

Mac arrives tomorrow.

Billie

NEW YORK CITY

Even after all these years, I still get a big buzz out of passing my thumb over the raised engraving on my business cards:

BILLIE ELROY-HOLLIS

ARTISTS' REPRESENTATIVE

Using Momma's maiden name worked out real well: has a nice ring to it. Every once in a while I send a slew of them along to Maryruth so she can pass them around to the folks in Evansville, and, sentimental though it may be, I keep the first one in a fourteen-karat-gold frame from Cartier on my desk, a permanent memento of the day I came into my own at last. Now, of course, I can be very choosy about taking on new clients—with my stable of stars I can afford to be. The only exception I've made recently is an artist who's had gallery shows in SoHo and also does commercial work—but not enough to suit me, because I've a hunch he could be a winner: Grafton Davis.

Garnet

"If you don't press charges, Janey, I will."

"You're hardly in a position to do that! Dear wasn't your cat."

"You seem to forget it happened in my house."

She fussed over the hot rollers for her hair, sulking about this for a while, and after a time said, "He's more impossible than ever since he got roped in by that bulldozer of an agent."

I let this go by without comment.

"She's the pushy take-over type—not a bit sweet like we are."

"Speak for yourself, Janey."

"Don't be sarcastic—it's most unbecoming."

"Well, so is your hanging on to Grafton."

"I'm not hanging on to him, I'm hanging on to you."

"Go back to him—that's what you really want."

"I wouldn't dream of doing that without you, Garnet."

Just then the phone rang and she ran to pick it up. "Oh—it's you," she said doubtfully. She listened without saying much, making little cooing sounds now and again. Then she slammed the phone down. "He wants me to meet her," she screamed. "Can you believe it?"

"The agent?" I said.

"Garnet, what'll I do? What'll I do? Her name's Billie!" she screamed, stamping her foot.

"Well, you can't do much about that, but I can. I'm leaving, Jane."

"You can't do that—"

"You and Grafton and this Billie person sound made for each other."

"But where are you going?"

"Nowhere, because you're the one going—this is my house, remember?"

I took her luggage (all eight satchels) from under the bed and her Bo-Peeps and Sadie Thompson satins from the closet and started neatly folding them into the suitcases.

"What are you doing?" she asked, starting to cry.

"Helping you pack," I said.

After a while her infallible sense of timing made her realize the tears wouldn't work—at least for the present—so she changed tactics, pulled herself up like Queen Mary and said calmly, with great dignity, "I can do that, Garnet. I don't want to be any more trouble to you than I've been already."

So she finished the packing on her own and I helped her with the suitcases. It took three trips up and down to get them out onto the sidewalk, and we stood there in the rain without an umbrella, waiting for a taxi.

After a long time, suddenly around the corner came the

longest limousine I'd ever seen. It was midnight blue, with smoky glass on the windows so you couldn't see inside, and instead of passing us by with the rest of the traffic it eased up to where we stood and stopped. A chauffeur in puce livery jumped out smartly, unfurling a large puce umbrella, and he opened the door of the limousine and out stepped Grafton. Behind him, in the back seat, wearing a coquettish hat of aigrette feathers, was a dumpy woman with a most efficient air about her. Grafton and the chauffeur piled the suitcases into the trunk of the car, and while this was being done, Jane stepped in and settled herself beside the woman on the back seat. Grafton stepped in after her, and the chauffeur shut the door, tipped his cap to me politely and drove away.

It had all taken place with great dispatch, with not a word said by any of us.

Billie

Honey Bear, I told Grafton, straight shooting, you've never realized your full potential as a commercial artist, and the real big money's in photography—think about that. So next thing I know, he brings a portfolio and what do you know? Seems he's been a photographer on and off over the years, just never put his mind to it. All I needed was to see his work to know this guy's got it. He's just been lollygagging along on top of a gold mine all these years, never knew what it is to be bitten by the BBB—Big Bucks Bug. Nothing impresses a client more than making something happen—fast—and I've already got him set for the *Glamour* account Scavullo turned down. This Davis guy's more like a movie actor than an artist type—loaded with personality, just doesn't know how to sell himself. He's tall and thin, with one of those English-type faces, aristocratic as they say, and eyes that look at people like he knows everything about them, even things they don't know themselves—things they might *like* to know. I can tell by the way he looks at me that he knows how sensitive I am underneath my business-wise exterior.

Jess

MOSCOW

We are breakfasting, Mac and I, in our sitting room at the Embassy—a breakfast with cheese and tea. The tea was brought in tall glasses on a birchwood tray and alongside is a bowl of strawberry jam with long enameled spoons (to spoon the jam into the tea, as much as we want). I had a dream last night about Dolores. She had been found, only I knew she wasn't my mother but an impersonator, and although the masquerade was skillfully devised and fooled others it did not fool me. I decided to tell Mac about the dream but kept putting it off. The minutes passed and now it's too late.

"She's a real leech, if you ask me," Mac is saying. He's talking about Brillianta, mumbling something about her wanting to come back with us to America, "can't wait to get her teeth fixed," and so on. "She has a point," he says, taking a big spoonful of strawberry jam and stirring it around in the tall glass. There is a silver band around the glass and a handle to hold it so that the hot tea doesn't burn. Still he says "Hot!" and puts the glass down. I lean over and brush my lips across his fingers.

"She tells everybody she's become like a daughter to Dolores—so you have an instant sister." He smiles.

"Thanks a lot," I say. And I move over to the sofa and stretch out, thinking about Katie, something she said once . . .

"I know what I'm going to do, Ma, when I grow up."

"What's that, darling?"

"Have a farm—in Connecticut—somewhere near the city but country, with lots of animals and cows I'll get from somewhere."

"Oh, that sounds lovely, Katie. And maybe there'll be a little room for me somewhere to come and visit."

"Oh, no, Darling Ma, you'll live with me—and it won't be a little room."

Mac looks over at me. "When does the doctor think your mother will be able to travel?"

"Next week. Perhaps. Who knows?"

"Is the nurse coming with her?"

"Of course Brillianta has offered herself for the job, but—"

"That's not a good idea," Mac says.

"No. She's too preoccupied with herself. I don't see her extending herself in the way nurses—the good ones, that is—have to."

"Still, Dolores does seem calmer when Brillianta's with her . . ."

My eyes start to sting and I close them, pressing my fingers into them until it hurts.

"I'll be with her." I turn away.

Mac is silent.

After a while he looks toward me. "What are you thinking?" he asks.

The phoebes call at dawn unanswered, I think, but I say, ". . . the way she was."

"You can't let go?"

"That's what I don't understand, because in some ways she's becoming the child and I the mother."

"She needs you now the way a child needs its mother."

"But how can I be that to her—when I still want a mother for myself."

"You were a mother—"

"I still am! Just because Katie's dead doesn't mean—"

"Sweetness—I didn't mean—"

"I know you didn't, Mac . . . but you're right—my life as a mother is over and I'm left longing more than ever for what Dolores was incapable of being even when I did have her—"

"You certainly gave to Katie what you never had."

"That's exactly it. So now Katie's dead and I keep trying to reach my mother and nobody's home—"

"I am—"

"I don't know who I am or where I belong."

"How about with me, Jessa?"

But do I?

Garnet

NEW YORK CITY

As a surprise for Jess when she gets back I'm working on a portrait of Katie—the way I remember her that day coming into the room, so alive and full of hope.

Sometimes I miss Jane. Other times when I'm working I never think of her although now and then I'll be starting a painting which takes on a life of its own and turns in one way or another into a portrait of her. Even the portrait of Katie baffles me— begins to look like Jane, forcing me to rub it out and start over. I really don't want to hear from her again, or see her. I want to belong to myself, the way I did long ago before I met Grafton and turned into someone else, someone I didn't know and certainly don't like. Claude calls every day but I put off seeing him. I don't trust myself with people yet, only with myself. Still I may see him soon. I'd respect myself a lot more if I could trust and love someone who I know would be good for me. Claude's a man who says what he means and means what he says. But I don't know if I'll ever be ready to let myself be at peace—happy. Although it's about time.

Jess

MOSCOW

Garnet dear,

Someone from the embassy here is flying to New York tonight and I'm asking him to post this to you from there otherwise God knows when you'll receive it.

As soon as Dolores is well enough to travel we'll be coming home. From her Diaries we now believe that Nicolai Voznesensky was responsible for her disappearance in 1933. Apparently he talked indiscreetly, boasting to my mother about what was happening, and then was afraid she might talk (as I may have told you, Dolores reacted violently to cruelty to animals). To save his career and her life, he had her kidnapped and committed in secret to a sanitarium. All my mother remembers is that she found herself in a strange place, with all communication with Voznesensky cut off and no way of contacting anyone. She still speaks of "Nico" as if he were alive.

I keep thinking about Katie—that she's waiting.

Love,
Jess

Brillianta Vosvi

There is no doubt in my logical mind that no matter how well intended she seems, the so-called daughter person is an impostor and will have to capitulate in the final moment and take me with her to America, for Dolores is onto her I can tell and will not set foot out of Moscow unless I am to accompany her. After all, we have had so many happy years together, side by side in the lovely Gorky—it would be most inappropriate to separate us now. I can afford to be civil, even friendly in outward appearance, to this Jessica impostor, for do not I have the upper hand, hold the ace of spades, haven't I caught the ring of gold and been crowned Queen of the May? Was it not I alone who cleverly freed Dolores by my wit and ingenuity, not to mention my teeth, which will be seen to first thing after we land on the earth of Manhattan Island? Jessica daughter chooses to believe I have not got her number, which is O.K. by me. Let her continue to do so, in whatever way makes her feel she has the upper hand. I know that she knows, and she knows that I know, who the *real* daughter is, but who the real Madre is, is anyone's guess.

Garnet

NEW YORK CITY

"Are you all right?" I said to Jess when she called.

She answered, "Yes, I think so."

She sounds much better, her voice stronger.

"Can I see you?"

"Yes, please. Can you come at five? And Dolores—you'll see her too."

Dolores recognized herself in me—I knew immediately—and I saw myself in her, but Jess was right: if you met her by chance you wouldn't know her.

"How do you do?" she said formally. "You remind me of someone I used to know . . ."

Jess said, "It's startling, isn't it, Mummy."

"Don't call me that," Dolores said, fluttering her hand in Jess's direction.

"I meant—Dolores." Jess smiled at me. "She doesn't like to be called Mother."

"Not by strangers," Dolores said huffily.

"How do you like America, Mrs. Willis?" I asked.

"I have a pretty room here, most suitable, although the bathroom could be larger—but the water's nice and hot, a welcome change from that other place I was visiting . . ."

"Dolores hasn't gone out yet, we're planning to any day now. I thought I'd take her to the botanical gardens."

"Yes, I do love flowers," Dolores said, staring at me. "What is your favorite flower?"

"Peonies," I said.

"Pink or white?"

"Both," I said.

Dolores nodded approval to Jess and said, "Such a pretty friend you have."

"Garnet's been looking forward to meeting you."

"Speaking of flowers," Dolores said, losing interest, "where's Brillianta?"

"She should be back any minute—she went shopping in Queens."

"Queens? I know of no queens in America," Dolores said, most put out.

"Don't worry, she'll be back soon."

"I'm not worried. I just don't like her out of my sight."

"But *I'm* here," Jess said almost angrily.

Dolores pretended not to hear.

"I'll bring you some flowers next time I visit, peonies if I can find them," I said. As I started to leave, in bustled a Mrs. Tittlemouse kind of person, bursting to tell Dolores about her adventures at the shopping mall in Queens.

"Thank you, Garnet, for coming," Jess said, following me out into the hall. "My mother tires easily, isn't quite sure of things yet, but we make progress . . ."

"Don't give out so much energy," I told her softly.

"I can't get used to having her in Katie's room."

"Then don't."

"But it's the only room she can have. I couldn't bear to have Brillianta Vosvi in Katie's room, so she's in the guest room and my mother's in Katie's."

"It's not how you thought it would be, is it?"

"I'm learning nothing ever is."

"I guess that's so . . ."

"Garnet, it's so strange, but there's someone who's been in my life for years and years, and when it happened—when Katie died—I never thought he'd be able to face it. But he did, and it's bringing me back to life . . ."

"Yes, of course! It must make all the difference—"

"He's with me in every way he can be, although he is married and I don't think Billie'll ever let him go."

"Billie? You mean Elroy-Hollis?"

Jess sighed. "I call her Bill, but it doesn't help things."

"It might help things sooner than you think," I said.

"What do you mean by that?"

But all I said was wait and see . . .

Things do finally fall like snow, like rain, gently, aptly into place.

Jess

Everything is quiet in the hour before the dawn as I enter the room—Katie's room—to sit in the chair beside her bed. The light starts its slow entry through the curtains as it did when she was little and had a cold and I'd sit beside her waiting for the fever to break. But it is not Katie who rests fitfully in this bed, it is my mother, and I wonder what her dreams are and what she will remember when she wakes. I breathe in and out slowly. Her eyes open as if she's heard me, and I say to her, "Are you all right?"

She looks toward me but says nothing. Perhaps she doesn't recognize who sits here beside her in the dark.

But she says, "I know you."

And I say to her, gently, "Who am I?"

And she says, "You're my friend."

As she says this I know that it could be true but if it were it would take a letting go that seals the heart and terminates the time of grief. Even if such could be, I don't want it. Just as I'll never let go of Katie, I'll never let go of Dolores, and even if in time she did become my friend I'd never say Good-bye to my mother, for the love that is lost is the love that is found and the love that lasts forever.

A NOTE ON THE TYPE

The text of this book was set in Goudy Old Style, one of the more than a hundred typefaces designed by Frederic William Goudy (1865–1947). Although Goudy began his career as a bookkeeper, he was so inspired by the appearance of several newly published books from the Kelmscott Press that he devoted the remainder of his life to typography, in an attempt to bring to the printers of the United States a better understanding of the movement led by William Morris.

Produced in 1914, Goudy Old Style reflects the absorption of a generation of designers with things "ancient." Its smooth, even color, combined with its generous curves and ample cut, marks it as one of Goudy's finest achievements.

Composed by PennSet, Inc.,
Bloomsburg, Pennsylvania

Printed and bound by Fairfield Graphics,
Fairfield, Pennsylvania

Designed by Dorothy S. Baker